CW01636115

THE PARSON

BY THE SAME AUTHOR

ASYLUM PIECE (stories)

A BRIGHT GREEN FIELD

CHANGE THE NAME

A CHARMED CIRCLE

EAGLES' NEST

I AM LAZARUS (stories)

ICE

JULIA AND THE BAZOOKA (stories)

LET ME ALONE

MERCURY

MY SOUL IN CHINA (novella and stories)

A SCARCITY OF LOVE

SLEEP HAS HIS HOUSE

A STRANGER STILL

WHO ARE YOU?

ANNA KAVAN

THE PARSON

PETER OWEN
LONDON AND CHESTER SPRINGS

PETER OWEN PUBLISHERS
73 Kenway Road, London SW5 0RE

Peter Owen books are distributed in the USA by
Dufour Editions Inc., Chester Springs, PA 19425-0007

First published in Great Britain 1995
This paperback edition published 2001
© The Estate of Anna Kavan 1995

All Rights Reserved.
No part of this publication may be reproduced in any form
or by any means without the written permission of the publishers.

This edition printed from a copy of the original typescript
held by McFarlin Library, University of Tulsa, Oklahoma, USA

ISBN 0 7206 1140 7

A catalogue record for this book is available from
the British Library.

Printed and bound in Great Britain by
Bookmarque Ltd, Croydon, Surrey

Publisher's Note

This is the only remaining novel by Anna Kavan, left among her manuscripts, which has never been published hitherto. A significant feature of the narrative is that it presages, through its undertones and imagery, some of her later and most enduring fiction. Some minor editorial emendations have been made to the final extant draft of the text prior to publication. Otherwise it remains unaltered, as the author wrote it.

It has not been possible to date the book exactly, but it was probably written between the mid-1950s and the early 1960s.

The Parson

1

ONE afternoon at the end of a wet northern summer, a most improbable meeting took place between two people from worlds which could hardly have been further apart.

One was a young lieutenant, the eldest of six children whose native country this was, and whose father had died long before, leaving the family in poor circumstances. The other, from the south, was like the heroine of a romantic story, beautiful and extremely rich.

Rejane had just left her current lover after a violent quarrel, meaning to stay away for a week or two, until her absence had reduced him to a sufficiently abject state. She was bored with all the usual places her set frequented, and had come to this northern country because she'd never seen it and it was the remotest place she could think of. But it rained the whole time and the hotel was empty. She was already planning to leave after a few days of solitary boredom when Oswald appeared, and she changed her mind.

The tall, athletic young man, whose skin was tanned much darker than his very fair hair, aroused her interest, not by his good looks but because she immediately saw that there was something puzzling about him, something incongruous, that required explanation.

He was unmistakably an army type; even now, in casual civilian clothes, the uniform could be felt in the background. And he had a certain military assurance, sure of himself as an officer and a gentleman, though without a trace of conceit or swagger. This, with his rather severe good looks and superb physique, made him unusually impressive for such a young man.

Yet it seemed to Rejane, unobtrusively watching him across the hotel room, that his assurance was slightly overstated, as if he needed to convince himself; and, suddenly, in one of the flashes of inspired intuition she sometimes had when her interest was aroused, she saw that it was only his position in life he was sure of – not of himself in the middle of it.

Most strange, this was to her, this division, as if he stood outside his own circumstances. Her interest was stimulated still further.

He looked so straightforward and normal, so extroverted. At a first glance, he seemed all simplicity and directness, a man made for action, not thought, engagingly natural and absolutely trustworthy, within his limitations. He should have been perfectly at ease with himself, entirely at home in his world. And, most of the time, he kept the assured army façade. Only at an occasional unguarded moment his face had a bewildered lost look that was touching and most unexpected. In his dark-blue eyes, to which his tropical tan gave a startling brilliance, could be seen the same lost bewilderment, so inappropriate it was almost uncanny, like an improbable secret he carried always upon his person.

Rejane wasn't touched by it, but she was intrigued. A secret was always a challenge to her, something she had to possess. On the spot, she decided to make this handsome walking secret her property, although it meant staying on here in the wilds, cut off from everything that composed her real existence. Five minutes ago, this small, out-of-the-way country had seemed a terrible bore, she'd wanted to leave by the very next boat. Now at last it had provided her with an interest – even the weather seemed to have turned over a new leaf.

*

The change in the weather was responsible for the whole thing. If this September day hadn't unexpectedly brought brilliant hot sunshine, she would never have seen Oswald at all. He would never have driven his mother across the moors to the comfortable little modern hotel where she was staying, which, during his absence abroad, had replaced the dilapidated smugglers' haunt he'd known all his life.

Though any stranger approaching across the moors would have supposed it to be miles inland, the hotel was really right on the edge of one of the countless inlets which turned the map of that coastline into a sort of fringe; deep narrow lochs, everywhere winding into the sombre landscape of moors and great granite tors.

As soon as the mother and son got out of the car, they could feel the pleasant salty astringency that rose from the unseen creek. Steep steps led down to a rough terrace of half-submerged rocks, around which the pellucid water, clear and solid looking as blue-green glass, lazily swelled and sank, to the barely perceptible rhythm of distant waves. While they were standing here, looking over the bright water to the upland slopes on the other side, a sudden chill penetrated the summery afternoon, as if sent to remind them that it wasn't *really* summer and that they were in the north, though the sun still shone and there wasn't a breath of wind.

So they went indoors and ordered tea in the hotel lounge; where they couldn't fail to be very much aware of the stranger who was its only other occupant, dressed with an elegant simplicity rarely seen in their sparsely populated district.

In the blond north, in that remote and unlikely setting, Rejane's dark beauty was quite extraordinary, with its sensuous contrast of pale flawless skin and almost black hair and eyes. Her complexion was pure magnolia. And her hair fell in soft, dark waves that always looked perfect and perfectly natural – everything about her had this inevitable sort of perfection, as if it just happened that way. Naturalness was one of her great assets, her beauty being in no way artificial, but the result of supreme good health. Her body was as perfect as Oswald's, and, though she was a few years his senior, might have belonged to a slim young girl – except that no young girl ever had so much glamour. The impression she liked to give – it was somewhat misleading – was of a charming and lovely girl, quite simple and unassuming, unspoiled by money and adulation.

To Oswald, she was by far the most enchanting person he'd ever seen. An irresistible attraction drew his eyes towards her; and he hardly tried to resist, as if such glamorous beauty must not be kept private but could be admired, like royalty, without rudeness.

His mother, too, though usually timid with strangers, seemed to feel free to observe this one, so different from herself. And, as if the contrast made her half aware of deficiencies in her own appearance, she vaguely pushed a stray wisp of hair under her ancient hat before picking up the teapot, which had been set in front of her. As she began to pour, still under the spell of the unknown beauty, she murmured, 'Who can she be? What can she be doing here? She doesn't look at all the sort of person to come to the moors. . . .' Then she stopped abruptly, silenced by her son's disapproving frown.

Though he'd always been deeply devoted to her, at this moment everything about his mother got on his nerves – her dowdiness, her sudden silence and meekness, as much as her muttered personal remarks. At the same time he felt guilty, unfair and unkind, knowing that devotion to her family was responsible for her behaviour – she was shy and awkward for the same reason that she was badly dressed; because the poverty that followed his father's death had limited her experience of the world, imprisoning her at home, so that she was out of her element in a hotel lounge, almost as if she belonged to a lower class than her handsome, obviously well-bred son.

*

It had been for him, the first born, rather than for any of his brothers and sisters, that she had saved and slaved, not only to educate him but to add to his share of the meagre patrimony, so that he could enter his father's regiment, as tradition required. In their small northern country, advanced in some ways, in others behind the times, it was still the age of absolute male supremacy, the divine right of the eldest son hadn't been questioned. So that Oswald could go into a crack regiment, the education of the younger boys had been skimped; the girls it had not been thought necessary to educate, beyond the rudiments their mother could teach them. This state of affairs Oswald himself found quite natural; but he'd never forgotten his debt, or that it was his duty to do credit to the family, as he always had done, coming back this time more of a credit to them than ever, already promoted, and assured of success in his profession – his superiors said he was sure to get to the top.

With his good looks, good manners and air of breeding, he might meanwhile have been enjoying a great success with the army ladies. But he'd never had any time for the flirtatious creatures who'd done their best to seduce him. Loyalty would have kept him away from them in any case; loyalty to his brother officers, and, still more, to his family, who had made sacrifices for his career – he valued it far too highly to risk a damaging scandal; and, anyhow, he was not attracted.

Because he always treated the women with the same cool politeness, and because he smoked and drank only in moderation and to be like his comrades, they called him The Parson, and the name stuck, being peculiarly appropriate. Even the men under him used it behind his back. In spite of his good fellowship and his natural zest for living, there really was something faintly priestlike about the fine-looking young man, which showed itself in his conscientiousness and integrity and in his dedicated attitude to the regiment. His little air of seriousness was distinctive and rather winning, and acted almost as an aphrodisiac on the spoiled, blasé women, bringing them around him like a swarm of bees.

They couldn't bear his imperviousness to their attractions. Just how impervious he was they never guessed, for he took care to hide the near-disgust they inspired in him physically, over-sexed as he considered them, over-stimulated by the climate and by good living. They couldn't leave him alone. But the more they pursued, the more distant he became. He really loathed the occasions when he was forced into contact with them. More than any unpleasant duty, he loathed the dances held at regular intervals, which he avoided at first, reading alone in his quarters, while his comrades disported themselves and conducted their more or less discreet intrigues.

The women were, of course, greatly in the minority, even the plainest of them much in demand; but the plethora of young partners didn't compensate for Oswald; they couldn't do without him. Finally they got the Colonel to assert his authority, on the grounds that for a junior officer to make himself conspicuous by not dancing showed intolerable conceit, and endangered regimental morale.

Ordered to attend, Oswald did so with the impeccable correctness with which he carried out all his duties, dancing with formal precision with each partner in turn, apportioning his time with scrupulous fairness, so that they all got equal shares. He hated the women now more than ever for forcing him to dance with them; hating above all things to feel, against his hard, fit, muscular body, their soft, yielding semi-nakedness, which always seemed to exude a lustful excitement repugnant to him beyond words. However, he had been given an order, so he had to obey it; always very correct, impersonal, as indifferent to his partner of the moment as if she'd been some piece of military equipment. At first this only inflamed his adorers. Yet, really, it *was* insulting, the way he let it be seen he hardly knew one of them from another. Circling the room with an expressionless face, holding the woman in his arms well away from him, he seemed to insult the very flesh of his partner. It was his way of getting his own back.

It was not unsuccessful. But he had to pay for it. In the long run it reacted against him. Though the husbands began by sniggering at the discomfiture of the wives they knew were unfaithful, they soon started to resent the implied insult to themselves – these, after all, were the women *they'd* chosen. And presently, when the women realized that Oswald never would succumb to their seductions, they turned nasty, trying to make trouble for him with their menfolk, creating unpleasant scenes, for which he, of course, got the blame. On the whole, he'd have aroused much less ill-feeling by presenting a new pair of horns all round. What would it have mattered, with the antlers they all wore already?

Since his virtue had made everybody uncomfortable, there was a consequent general withdrawing, a cooling-off towards him, his popularity in the mess suffered a sharp decline, and his nickname, The Parson, came to be used more as a sneer. The really senior officers still thought highly of him; the CO, particularly, valued his dedicated attitude which belonged to a past generation of soldiers, already almost extinct. The older women too remained friends with him, and he with them. There was nothing of the woman-hater in his temperament. On the contrary, it was his idealized notion of womanhood that made the promiscuous sexiness of the young wives so repulsive to him.

For his age, time and position, he was singularly innocent – it was part of his charm – without being in any way prudish, priggish or epicene. His attitude towards sex was rather romantic; he had too much regard for it to degrade it by sordid little affairs and mean escapades. He wasn't a virgin, but confined his activities to the meek brown women smuggled intermittently into the officers' quarters. And there was always the sublimation of exercise. Often, at the end of an exacting day, while his companions relaxed over their drinks, he would be out on his sweating polo pony on the parched *maidan*, practising alone in a cloud of dust, until it got too dark to see the ball.

The army was everything to him, any other sort of existence unthinkable. As long as he'd been accepted in friendliness by his equals, he'd lived untroubled, unthinking, content with his humble but essential place in the structure of the regiment. Only now, in the time of his unpopularity, he began to feel lonely and dissatisfied. He'd given himself absolutely to the discipline of the regiment, and his loyalty couldn't be shaken. But simply to know he was doing his duty seemed not to be enough. His former thoughtless, almost childish content was no longer possible. He had to think about the way he'd been made to feel isolated, different from his companions; and, as soon as he started thinking, he saw that they'd turned against him unfairly, simply because he'd kept to his principles.

He'd never been lonely before. Good-natured as he was, equable and a natural athlete, popularity had always been his as a matter of course. A slight unconscious sense of inferiority on account of his northern origin had prevented him from making any close friends in the regiment – inevitably he was out of touch with the ideas and opinions the others freely expressed. But, really, he'd felt no need of intimacy, existing always in a group. He'd been satisfied with the rather desultory superficial contact he had with his comrades. Now, suddenly, this was lost to him, he was left stranded.

He assumed indifference and assurance to cover his loneliness. His physical condition was perfect, and nobody must suspect that there was anything wrong with him inwardly. Since he was not introspective, his unsatisfactory state remained for the most part unthought about, undefined. But he knew that all was not well with him. Gradually he developed a nameless sort of yearning, a vague dream of easement, never put into words. And sometimes, listening, under the hot evening sky, to the men singing sentimental songs he had heard at home, he felt restless and sad, stirred by his vague longings.

Only a woman, he knew instinctively, could satisfy them; but none of those accessible to him were sympathetic; so his confused, inarticulate unhappiness became fixed, tolerable because of its definite limitation. Everything would come right again when he went on leave, back to his home and to his mother, he was sure of that. He had always been perfectly happy to spend all his free time with her, never wanting anyone else, even after he'd joined the regiment.

Throughout the voyage home he was dreaming of her, looking forward to their meeting; to a renewal of their close mutual understanding.

Yet, just precisely this time, when he came back after the years of absence, needing her more than he'd ever done since childhood, there seemed no understanding, everything was changed. *She* seemed changed, older, further away; they seemed to have grown apart. He found he could no longer confide in her as in the past. It was a terrible disappointment to him. He was left with his undefined grievance, his dissatisfaction, of which he became much more conscious, without the distraction of duty and discipline that had kept him going.

All at once, his predicament seemed far more grave, since he could see no end to it. And it seemed so unfair, when all the time he'd been doing his duty in uncongenial circumstances – as a northerner, he'd always hated the tropical heat. Surely he deserved something, after the years of exile? Something of the dream that had touched him when the soldiers sang in the brief moment before the night, and the smoke rose in straight lines, diaphanous, pungent, into the cloudless sky?

His dream was too indefinite to put into words; perhaps no more than the desire to feel at ease again in his life; he knew only that it had failed to materialize. And his home, where nothing was as he had so confidently expected and believed it would be, had failed him.

His brothers had grown up and departed to various jobs; two of his sisters were married and living in distant towns. That left only Vera, the most intelligent and least attractive of the girls, the one he liked least, the one doomed, apparently, to a life of frustration as companion of his mother in her declining years.

As soon as the excitement of his arrival was over, disappointment engulfed him. Since the contact with his mother was broken and couldn't be mended, there seemed no point in their being together. In spite of their mutual love, the years relentlessly kept them apart. When he answered her questions, he was all the while conscious that she really wanted something more personal than the objective account of his travels that was all he could, or would, give her, feeling – without ever quite allowing the thought to form – that this was all of him she was now able to understand.

His home was very isolated, high up on the moors, miles from any large town. There were no distractions, apart from a few boring visits to scattered neighbours. As things were, he could see no sense in staying on there, and began to make vague plans for getting away.

His sister meant very little to him, a big serious girl who seldom spoke, and whose presence he accepted very much as he accepted the furniture he had known all his life; until she astonished him by saying she knew what he had in mind – it was just like him to go off to enjoy himself, leaving her stuck here with her mother on this godforsaken moor.

Startled by her criticism, Oswald told himself she was warped and bitter because she'd been condemned, practically, as the last unmarried girl, to stay here as long as the old woman lived. But it was such a commonplace of their society, it was always happening, he couldn't take it very seriously. Her bitterness, anyway, seemed excessive; and why should it be directed against him?

It took him some time longer to find out that what Vera really resented was his acceptance of the money essential to his career, which she helped her mother to earn by doing odd jobs of sewing and preserving and so on, for their richer acquaintances. He'd never even thought about it before. The family tradition required the eldest son to enter his regiment, which necessitated a private income of some kind: therefore an income must be provided for him – it was as simple as that – and, if it could be provided in no other way, so it must be. Now appalling vistas of doubt opened up.

His sister said frankly that it annoyed her to see him taking everything as his right – he should realize what was being done for him – and now let the subject drop. Neither of them ever mentioned it again. But of course it went on working in Oswald's mind. Not only had he been made to feel guilty but put under an obligation he could neither end nor discharge, since he couldn't think of leaving the army.

So much for his idea of going away, which now became impossible, an act of monstrous ingratitude he could not contemplate for a moment. Instead, he rather grimly set himself to make amends, devoting himself to his mother, trying to please her in everything.

But it was not a success. Consciously, the old lady understood nothing of what was going on under the surface: though she was grateful and proud to be seen about with her handsome son, so much attention embarrassed her. Feeling the hidden strain, she would have preferred to be treated in the old offhand way that seemed natural to her, and left at home.

Oswald's efforts began to seem rather futile, as it became clear that he was unable to make her happy – his own unspoken grievances saw to that, making him feel on edge, so that he experienced more and more often the irritation that had twitched at his nerves when she spoke of Rejane.

*

Her presence was a point of anxiety in him now, preventing his thought from concentrating upon the unknown woman across the room. For a second, when he glanced at the stranger, his dream seemed to hover near, an indescribable brightness, spreading wings of promise, of peace. All he wanted was to sit quietly near the woman who had evoked his dream. But, all the time, he had to consider his mother. At any moment she would start fussing, saying they must start for home.

Suddenly a soldier's automatic awareness of weather conditions made him look out of the window. A peculiar blanching and blurring process was obscuring the light outside. The sun was paling, a curious dimming was everywhere apparent, pallor was diffusing itself into the air, smudging the shapes and stealing the colours of the garden flowers. Eclipsed to a pale lamp, the sun abruptly went out altogether; the cliff withdrew from sight. Only a few of the flowers in the foreground still floated, dim and derealized, colourless ghosts of themselves, in the thick white mist billowing up from the invisible water, which could be heard softly sucking and smacking the rocks below.

All solid reality was now contained by the room, the world outside obliterated by this nebulous whiteness steaming up from the creek. In a sudden childish fantasy Oswald saw it as a screen, behind which the hidden rocks, the flowers, the water, were working to help him attain his dream, that undefined shimmering thing, out of reach, but nearer than it had been, no longer utterly inaccessible.

His mouth softened and lost its sternness. Suddenly he looked younger, boyish, again. Now he was as he should have been all the time, with a more natural confidence, and something altogether warm and winning about him. Feeling happier than for a long time, he leaned back, stretching out his long legs, fully relaxed in his chair for the first time since he'd sat down there.

His natural warmth, which the army trouble had almost suppressed, was restored to him. Now he saw his mother's face as pathetic instead of provoking, and was filled with compassion for her. Eager to show her how much he still loved her, he said with an affectionate smile, 'It looks as if we're here for the night.'

'For the night . . .?' She was sitting with her back to the window, and had anyhow been far away in some daydream of her own, from which she returned in confusion, not understanding.

'Look out of the window.'

Instead of doing as she was told, she gazed fixedly at him, astonished by the change, recognizing the humorous, playful look and voice of the past. Her heart began beating fast in joyful excitement. Her beloved son seemed suddenly to have come back to her as he used to be, in his true self, as he hadn't been since his return. But, even as she looked fondly into his face, where the old, easy, smiling charm had replaced irritation and sternness, in the background was the hurting fear that he might revert to what he had seemed before. So, controlling herself, she looked over her shoulder. And at once the rolling whiteness outside put her into a nervous flutter.

'Fog! Why didn't you tell me sooner? But I ought to have guessed from the way it suddenly turned cold. . . . We'll have to hurry back before it gets any worse. . . .'

Already, while still speaking, she had collected her modest possessions, and now she quickly stood up, her anxious eyes looking down at Oswald, lounging in his chair, smiling, and clearly not intending to move an inch.

'It's quite bad enough for me as it is,' he answered her lightly, 'so you might just as well sit down again.'

'But Vera's expecting us back to dinner. . . . She'll be wondering . . .'

'Then you'd better ring up and explain.'

He leaned back, smilingly assuming from some mysterious reservoir of forgotten disguises the mischievous sly look, with which, as a little boy, he had always charmed her, and which he knew she still couldn't resist.

'It may clear in a minute,' she weakly protested, wanting to be reassured, not about the weather, but that he was indeed the one who'd seemed unaccountably lost to her.

'It may, or it may not.' He was consulting his watch. 'We couldn't get back in daylight, possibly. And I'm not risking fog-pockets up on the moors in the dark – not even for you.'

Playful, engaging, casual, he refused to be serious, yet was fixed in his masculine will to stay. The affectionate, teasing voice tugged at her heart. But she had been so hurt, she understood so little, she was afraid to believe in the magical transformation, saying at random, 'You really think it would be dangerous?'

Stretched out there, immovable as a rock, relaxed and solemnly teasing, he replied, 'I do', disguising his impatience. Knowing the pathetic cause of her hesitation, he gazed at her gently, deliberately charming her to accept her own happiness, all irritation gone out of him and forgotten.

'Very well. I'll go and telephone Vera.' With a little ecstatic sigh the mother surrendered finally, incapable of further resistance. By some miracle her darling had been restored to her, all the more precious because he had seemed lost. As she crossed the room she looked back several times, hardly able to let him out of her sight, in case he again disappeared. She idolized him, absolutely, he could do no wrong; therefore the past unhappiness must be her fault, though she didn't see how. . . .

*

At last the door closed behind her, and Oswald was free to give his whole attention to the lovely pale face, framed by smooth dark hair, of which, all the time, he had been intensely aware, establishing, while he talked to his mother, a curious silent understanding with the unknown woman. Though seeming to take no notice of Rejane, he had known, through his acute consciousness of her, that she was listening to their conversation – it was almost as if she had been included in it. So it now seemed quite natural that she should ask, 'Is it really dangerous to drive in this?' With a slightly foreign gesture that he found charming, she indicated the fog, as she got up and went to stand at the window.

'Yes, it can be dangerous on the moor.' Oswald stood up too and approached her. 'It's easy to miss a turning, or to get off the road altogether.'

To his delight, everything seemed easy and natural. And, as he came to stand at her side, with the dramatic effect of a curtain going up for their special benefit, the dense whiteness parted outside, momentarily revealing a strange grey world of ghost vegetation, quenched and unearthly, every cold leaf and petal running with moisture as if under water, before it descended again.

'How long will it last?'

Not noticing the frown that accompanied the question, Oswald said cheerfully, 'No one can tell you that – another two minutes, perhaps. Perhaps another two days.'

'One might really be stuck here for two whole days? . . . Not able to get away?'

Now he had to meet Rejane's incredulous indignant look; a look almost of consternation, the mere notion of being detained forcibly by something she couldn't control being intolerable to her self-willed nature, which, since childhood, had known no restraint or coercion.

Taken aback and uncomprehending, he made some vague reply, out of his depth suddenly, his confidence abruptly shattered. In all his life no woman had ever moved him like this one, who had brought his dream into the room. But she was receding visibly, and anxiety seized him: he had only these few flying seconds, before his mother returned, in which to establish a bridge to the lovely stranger. Hearing her say, as if following her own thoughts to a conclusion, 'That settles it. I *shall* go on the next boat', he was really alarmed, exclaiming, 'Oh, but you mustn't!' horrified by the prospect of losing the wonderful being he'd only just found, watching her nervously, while she murmured, as if to herself, 'I should never have come here at all.'

'My mother said you weren't the sort of person to come to the moors.'

Why did he have to waste time on such a futile remark, when there wasn't a second to lose? However, to his immense relief, it seemed to recall her attention.

'Did she say that? How strange. . . .'

Though Rejane clearly saw more in the words than he did, he dismissed his mother with 'She's good at fortune-telling and all that . . .', continuing hastily, 'You can't have seen much, with all this rain, can you?' Without giving her time to answer, he went straight on: 'Some parts of the moor are magnificent, it's got a beauty of its own – out of this world. But visitors hardly ever see the best places because they're so hard to get at. But I shouldn't think you'd mind that. I wouldn't expect you to like things that were too easy.' The last words were prompted by a sense of urgency; but, having spoken them, he looked at her doubtfully – had he introduced the personal note too soon? He gazed intently into her face as if in search of a revelation.

Rejane looked back at him with her unchanging, almost black eyes, in which no expression was legible, although she was watching him with a new interest. Strange how he suddenly seemed to have come alive, thrown off some repressive burden. This sudden emergence of intensity and imagination, in conjunction with his solid, manly good looks, was surprising and totally unforeseen. His face, animated now, had that touch of seriousness that had so captivated the army wives – she too found it attractive.

'What have you seen so far?' he was meanwhile asking, encouraged by her attentive regard. 'Isap Tor, I suppose, and the Five Falcons and Roko. All very nice and neat, tidied up for the summer tourists, but not the real moor at all.' Loneliness had intensified his feeling for the countryside round his home, so that it was easy for him to speak of the moor without any self-consciousness. 'I could show you wonderful places that are sheer magic. But you wouldn't be able to drive there because there aren't any roads – just heather and bracken and rock and the sea creeping in where you least expect it. In the old legends the sea is always at war with the tors, trying to undermine them. But those towers of rock won't fall until the last judgement. They'll always be standing there like besieged fortresses, never falling, old as the earth itself, fixed in their places like the sky and the waters under the earth.'

He had a very agreeable soft voice, almost a singer's voice in its delicate, slow inflections; and now it had unconsciously assumed a slight singsong lilt, imitated from the local story-tellers of his childhood. Suddenly he heard it, heard what he was saying, and stopped, slightly embarrassed, as he always was by the sensitive, imaginative self he kept battened down out of sight beneath layers of masculine toughness, only fully aware of it when, as now, it had dangerously exposed itself.

This time there was no danger, apparently; Rejane was looking at him with evident interest. But his practical self had come uppermost, and, determined to persuade her before his mother interrupted them, he said coaxingly, 'Do stay a bit longer and let me show you something of the real moor.'

She'd already made up her mind to stay, but she said nothing yet. It amused her to watch the delicacy with which, not presuming to touch her, by way of emphasis he laid the tips of his fingers gently on the book she was holding. And his northern voice was fascinating when he was being intense, with its queer singing undertone and extraordinary flexibility; unimagined depths of softness were in it now, almost a coo. She smiled to herself faintly, though she still said nothing.

Her silence was beginning to seem hopeful to him. Now, suddenly, in the midst of his pleasant excited feelings, came one so singularly inappropriate that it distracted him for the length of time he took to wonder why in heaven's name a danger signal should have gone up in his mind, as if warning him not to go any further. He forgot about it at once, and went on with his pleading: 'Don't be frightened away by the fog. Look, it's lifting already!'

The world outside was in fact reappearing, though minus a dimension, as if made of water, frequented only by the ghosts of things as they were under the sun. Looking back at Rejane, he hoped wildly that she would say yes. The calm magnolia-mask of her face did not change, nor did her jewel-dark eyes, their fluttering fans of lashes long and soft as a sable paintbrush. Unkindly keeping him in suspense, only at the very last, when they'd both heard his mother's approaching step, she gave him a slight, smiling nod.

Unconscious of any unkindness, he was overwhelmed by a wonderful thrill of joy he could hardly conceal, and in a warm, vibrant voice said to the old woman coming into the room, 'You must help me describe our moors – we can't have people going off without appreciating them, can we?'

His mother was a little bewildered by these rapid developments. She'd have liked to keep the son she adored to herself, for a time at least. But whatever he wanted was right, and she wanted it too. Though slightly overawed by the beauty and obvious wealth of this new acquaintance, she was ready to make friends, accepting Rejane as she'd have accepted a Hottentot, had Oswald wished it; for he was her idol, and his will was law.

2

SO the improbable relationship started between the young officer and the guest at The Hope Deferred, the unworldly devoted mother hovering very much in the background. The young man was supremely happy. The situation was just what he wanted, exactly what seemed needed for his happiness. At last he could get rid of that awful sense of being isolated and injured. His dream at last took a definite shape and he knew what he wanted, which, of course, was Rejane.

As if the forces of nature really were on his side, there was no more fog or rain, no more thundery heat, but a long sequence of brisk, bright autumn days, just the weather he liked best, when the moors looked their best. And, as this fine weather seemed sent to compensate for the bad summer, Oswald believed that his former unlucky period had been succeeded by one more fortunate, when virtue would be rewarded instead of penalized, according to what he'd been taught.

Uplifted by a mixture of pride, happiness and excitement, he drove Rejane to lunch at his home. He was aware, as he had not been for a long time, of the sheer joy of being alive, and of the beauty of the day and of the world. It gave him intense pleasure to drive through the pale, thin, autumn sunshine, with her sitting beside him, as serene and lovely as the sky itself, talking as easily as if they'd been old friends. It seemed to him that everyone they passed on the road – most of them people he'd known all his life – must be envying him and admiring his companion.

Out of his pride a more elusive feeling grew up which he

couldn't have named. It made him regard her rather as though she were a royal princess who had been entrusted to his care. When, after gazing at the enormous view, floating in floods of luminous sunshine, she exclaimed, 'How lovely it is here!', at the same time lightly touching his arm, a tremor of deep emotion went through him. He longed to press her hand to his lips, but found that he derived even more satisfaction from *not* doing so, proud to feel himself trusted, looking at her with respect and profound devotion. At the same time, something impelled him to wonder how much of the beautiful day would be left to him if she were not there. He realized suddenly, almost with alarm, that his own heightened enjoyment was due to her presence, and to the unspoken intimacy that seemed to be growing between them.

*

They drove at first through a sheltered valley where summer still lingered, a sprinkling of yellow leaves hardly noticeable in the dense green of the big trees, oaks, ashes and elms. Towards midday the sun was still strong, and they passed whole families round the scattered farmsteads, bringing in the last crop of the season.

Then, as the road climbed up to the moors, the softer characteristics of the landscape gradually vanished, widening stretches of heath alternating with rough, dry-walled fields, until all cultivation ceased. Here, on the higher more exposed ground, the bracken was turning gold, and, from thickets of slighter trees, birches and aspens, leaves came spinning down in golden showers.

Soon a sea of silence, sunshine and solitude stretched around them in every direction to the tors, bunched spectrally on the horizon, the undulating expanse of heather and pale, plumy grass breaking out here and there in sprays of purple and golden brown. Trees became fewer and fewer, there were more and more outcroppings of pale granite: and to this sunlit desert the sudden brilliant flash of water came startlingly, like a vision. Ghostly looking yet monumental, the distant tors seemed to float in the sky; while lesser, nearer masses of stone and boulders were strewn about everywhere, some quite near the road, their pockets full of delicate little ferns and cushions of emerald velvet moss. Always climbing, the road grew rougher and narrower, finally reduced to a stony track, along which the powerful car – hired for the duration of Oswald's leave – swayed and jolted uneasily. It was quite impossible to keep up any speed.

Rejane looked about, rather amazed to find herself so far outside civilization, though Oswald had already explained that he lived near the last village of all, beyond which there were no roads, and that this one came to an end at his house.

'Nearly there,' he now told her, smiling and reassuring.

There was something oddly comforting in the way he seemed to watch over her all the time, always watchful for her well-being, standing guard over her, with perfect correctness and old-fashioned courtesy – courtliness, rather – surrounding her with his warm masculine kindliness and protective devotion, which was really rather charming. And there was something else about it, more important to her than charm.

*

Her pleasing unaffected façade, the pretence that all her beauty and wealth made her no different from other people, concealed the implacable underside of her character, and an obsession with self that was truly phenomenal. Some lingering narcissism left over from her solitary childhood had combined with the universal admiration she'd received later to create in her mind a glorified self-image. With a part of her, anyhow, she half believed in herself as a kind of superior being, almost as though she possessed supernatural powers. The real power, of course, was the power of her money, as her rational self knew quite well. But she'd played all her life at being a queen or an enchantress in secret, so that it *almost* seemed true. Oswald's reverential attitude was important because it played up to this unreal reality and made it seem more like truth. She'd never before met anyone who flattered her dream-self as he did, so that she really felt she belonged on a pedestal or a throne. To feel his male deference paying tribute to her all the time, with a sort of knightly chivalry, was immensely gratifying to her obsession.

But, as her rational self, she wanted to laugh at the strange young man who was falling in love with such solemn intensity. She knew he was already in love with her by his reaction to her touch; which also suggested that he was afraid of love in the physical sense, and so made her into a goddess to be worshipped from far away. It was just what her queenly enchantress-self wanted, but her real self almost burst out laughing; she, Rejane, to be worshipped from afar – it was too funny. . . .

Quick as the darting of a snake's tongue, she darted at him a sidelong glance of cynical southern disillusionment, a look of somewhat sinister mischief flickering on her face, which, for that instant, for all its loveliness, looked malevolent, witchlike.

That there was something witchlike about her, Oswald's instinct had told him, warning him off. He had ignored the warning, already infatuated by this dangerous charmer; but if he'd seen that inhuman look of mocking, cold-blooded amusement, his chivalrous soul might have taken fright. However, he was unsuspecting and saw nothing. Not for one moment did he suspect what he was bringing with him as, turning a sharp corner, he pointed upwards and on to his home.

At the gesture, and his exalted expression, Rejane, not quite out of her witch-self, exclaimed silently, 'Excelsior!' – the look of heartless mockery flickering again. But immediately afterwards she was surprised into a very different frame of mind.

Still climbing, they'd been for the last few minutes in a cleft between stony slopes of heather and bracken, nothing else to be seen; she'd no idea they were near the summit. So she was disconcerted to see, straight above them, the hoary grey head of rock, thrust into, and filling the sky. Taking her by surprise, the bare upheaval of naked granite, grim and overwhelming in its immensity and nearness, had a strong effect on her imagination. She'd never been close to one of the tors; and, to her surprised eyes, there was something extraordinary about that huge knot of pale, up-ended stones, towering aggressively just overhead, like a fortress, excluding the sun.

The track curved, crumpled folds of distant moorland reappeared, other tors rearing up dimly, one behind another, rocky islands in the vast sunlit sea. But always this near mass of granite loomed close above, between them and the sun, *too* close, it seemed to her – it made a chilling impression. Though there was nothing here to compare with the scenic grandeurs she'd seen in various parts of the globe, the unexpectedness of it impressed her. What a weird place, she thought, and, connecting it with the man at her side, What a truly astounding place to call home! – meaning the pile of boulders up there, not the house she hadn't yet seen.

Her imagination was already at work weaving the tor into a fantasy of her own; she had to do this, or it would seem too overpowering. She was thinking that nature, surely, had never produced that heap of rocks, which looked clumsy and awkwardly balanced, and to her had an eerie, impossible aspect, unlike the work of man, either – more like some half-wit giant's attempt at building. Her dramatic eye saw it as the product of an unsuccessful experiment in evolution, as if an extinct race of crazy titans had left this evidence of their failure before perishing from the earth. She actually seemed to feel the lingering emanation of their resentment. Evoked by her imagination, an aura of ancient malice seemed to cling, even now, to the gruesome great stones. By substituting her own invention, this ghostly malevolence of prehistory, she came to terms with whatever it was had impressed her.

'How do you like our tor?' Oswald asked, turning his blond head to beam at her warmly and protectively – he might as well have beamed protectively at a tiger.

'Wonderful!' she smiled back, amused by him again. He seemed so blissfully unaware of her as she really was. But she was curious, too. There was the element of mystery about him – how could there *not* be, born and bred as he had been in the shadow of that mysterious house of demons up there? She'd only just seen *his* house, on top of a smaller hill in the foreground, because of the dominant effect of the crag, standing straight above it. It was built of the same pale stone and looked cold and forbidding, but was overshadowed, actually and metaphorically, in spite of its size and position, by the other ominous edifice higher up.

In front, a wilderness of a neglected garden ran downhill to a shallow, fast-running brown stream, glinting among its stones; and directly behind, the moor jutted steeply, crowned by those weirdly piled rocks, which Rejane had endowed with the spells of prehuman erectors. Her fantasy had the side-effect of making Oswald more interesting, more of a puzzle to her. She couldn't imagine what sort of man he could be, having lived in the shade of that antique malice; but she meant to find out.

She said no more to him then. And he was satisfied, for he saw that she was impressed, and knew intuitively that what impressed her was the atmosphere of the place, for which he himself had such a strong feeling. As a child, he'd always been fascinated by the old stories about the moor. Something of childhood magic lived on in him even now, though he could never have expressed the sense of wonder, of something heroic, splendid and remote, that so entranced him, like a glimpse of a legendary, lost golden age. He'd never spoken about it to anyone, not even to his mother, always feeling no one would understand. It seemed miraculous, and yet perfectly natural, that Rejane should come straight into his secret world, where all was silent, dreamlike, beyond description. Her silence was perfect to him, his own thoughts could not have been spoken. He drove in a kind of ecstatic trance, while she amused herself with her race of imaginary premen, half magicians, but doomed to extinction because their development had taken a wrong twist. Their resentment had spun a venomous web of magic to last as long as the rock into which they'd infused it. The story she'd invented already seemed real – her new pretence-life, it was to be.

It was strange, she was so assured and poised, her confidence seemed unshakeable. Yet she had occasional rare moments of insecurity. She liked a man to stand between her and the world, to relieve her of its full impact. In the same way, she preferred acting a part to real living – imaginary worlds being more manageable than the real one. But the deception was barely conscious. Once her mind had accepted a pretence, it became her reality, for the time being. So now the world she had left behind began to seem hazy, unreal. Even the lover's face became indistinct. Though she had no intention of losing him, for the present he faded out, replaced by this northern world, so entirely different, with the tor looming ominous in the sky, and her ghostly prehumans.

Oswald of course was to introduce her to this strange north; the icy, demonic, alien north she so far only imagined as lying in wait, like a presence, behind the superficial appearance of civilization. She'd endowed him with some of her invented magic, which must have entered into him, living in the shadow of those old stones. That was why he was able, as no one else ever had been, to make her feel a princess. So it all fitted together.

She would act with him, outside her normal existence, a brief interlude, based on the mystique of the moor, all rather uncanny in the hushed northern strangeness. But of its essence only an interlude, nothing lasting about it. She'd found out that he was due to return to duty in just over a month, so that was all right. She could put in a month as a sort of poetic child of the northern moors quite happily. And the lover would wait that long. Let him wait. It would teach him a lesson.

So, without his knowledge, Oswald's fate was decided. As

though feeling her thoughts upon him, he turned his head, but at once had to look back at the road.

He was very much the gallant, chivalrous lover, and quick as a woman, almost, to detect her moods. In his deep-blue eyes, which were incapable of deception, could be read an endless tenderness and devotion; though whether he'd ever dare to approach her as a man was open to doubt. It didn't matter. She always rather shrank from a man, physically, though she'd taught herself to enjoy the embraces of men. What was much more important to her at the moment was the glimpse she'd just caught of that incongruous sort of misgiving – a curious hollow look of uncertainty which was a puzzle to her, and a stronger attraction than all his good looks and other qualities put together.

*

The car tilted over a humpback bridge, crossing the stream, flat stepping-stones at the side for people on foot to cross the brown busy water – like crossing into the Middle Ages, it seemed to Rejane – and climbed steeply on between jungles of flowering plants gone back to the wild, convolvulus smothering everything, blowing its trumpets triumphantly everywhere after the wet season, although its leaves were already beginning to droop and wither, touched by the frost.

The house seemed not only at the end of the road but at the end of the world. The engine of the car was switched off and silence descended, into which Rejane stepped out – into this absolute northern silence, timeless, as if everything had stopped, and they'd come, not to the Middle Ages but to a place before time began. If there was a village near it must have been on the other side of the hill, for not a single habitation was visible in the whole huge encirclement of the moors.

In miles, the distance they'd come from The Hope Deferred wasn't very great; yet everything here seemed oddly different, changed. Besides the new silence and solitude, there was a new coolness. The upland air was sharp, even in sunshine. And that the place had already turned towards winter was evident, not only in the overgrown garden but in the pale sear grass slope above, reaching up, between frequent knots and ridges of granite, to the pale looming mass of stone; and in the faint blue, hardly blue at all, of the sky.

In its silence, particularly, the vast, pale, deserted landscape, with its bare islands of ghostly rock, seemed to her to exhale something hostile to human life, stony and arid, without sound or movement, a lifeless and empty scene. In the almost frightening silence she saw the house as the advance-post of some doomed expedition, recklessly daring the curse of that wintry region, already lying upon it in the shadow of the rocks overhead, balanced in precarious-seeming immensity, threatening to fall and crush it out of existence.

But the interior of the house was less romantic, merely gloomy and dark, with the peculiar petrified gloom of houses that have known better days, where people live in the past. The cold rooms seemed damp, and gave the impression of being arranged as they had been twenty or more years before. The furniture was massive, dark and heavy, the pictures hung darkly and obscurely upon the walls, between military trophies, banners, helmets, sabres; the rust on the steel looked like bloodstains, the dusty, bedraggled plumes on the helmets suggested that the curse had come home to roost.

In this dismal atmosphere the lunch wasn't very successful, though Rejane was charming as usual. And the old lady did her best, ingenuously, childishly chattering about people and things the visitor had never heard of; until she forgot, and sat staring blankly, out of those queer psychic eyes that seemed to see only ghosts. Then, with a guilty glance at Oswald, she would start up again, scattering her inconsequent sentences into a gulf of incomprehension thousands of miles across.

They were an odd trio of women sitting at lunch, around the correct, handsome young man. The dreamy-eyed mother seemed scarcely present, despite her spasms of conversation. And he was there only for Rejane. His sister, tall, flushed, with an air of suppressed resentment, made frequent trips to the kitchen, hardly saying a word.

The elegant, worldly Rejane sat through the meal in her amused casual fashion, finding it all rather boring, rather an imposition. Why should she, who must never be bored, put up with these absurd people? Oswald should have known better than to bring her here.

She was thankful when the meal was over at last, and they could go, leaving the house with almost indecent haste. Once she was alone in the car with him, her habitual good humour returning, she could smile at the memory of those cold, disastrous rooms.

Although to the man they were simply 'home', a background he wouldn't have dreamed of criticizing on his own account, so familiar he never really looked at them, he had seen that they were not for her. He at once proposed that in future they should meet at the hotel; a far better arrangement from his point of view, its great advantage being that he'd have her to himself, instead of having to share her with his mother and sister. Thank goodness for the fast car, and the freedom it gave him.

3

WHILE Rejane's interlude progressed to her satisfaction, Oswald found it less satisfactory, in spite of spending whole days alone with her, in the providentially fine weather, exploring the moors. Many of the wild beauty spots were remote, and could be reached only on foot, or by riding the rough-coated, sure-footed ponies that roamed the district, belonging to no one, or to any landowner who took the trouble to claim and train them.

The young cavalryman of course had always ridden himself, and was delighted to find Rejane equally at home on horseback. His naïve optimism took it as a sign that they were meant for each other. With extreme care he chose her a good-looking, dark-brown pony, with long, creamy mane and tail, which they called Coffee. And every morning they would set off with a picnic lunch, riding up to the moors.

The young man was at his best there, confident and at home, as if the whole wild landscape were his demesne, to which he welcomed her as an honoured guest, bestowing its freedom upon her, and making himself responsible for her safety and happiness; always attentive, devoted, surrounding her with his watchfulness, ready to avert any contretemps before it could occur. If her pony stumbled, slipped on the shelving rock-face, or went too near one of the treacherous patches of bog, he was always there, with his unobtrusive helpfulness and constant, undemanding devotion. She marvelled at his capacity for unselfish and loving service; and much more, at his lack of interest in her income.

She found this one of the most puzzling things about him.

No one, in her whole life, had allowed her to forget, as he did, how rich she was – her wealth had always been an important factor in her relations with others. She was so used to the sincere respect people had for her money that she could hardly believe in Oswald's indifference, and, when finally she became convinced, she despised him slightly for being so unmercenary. A little store of contempt was accumulating somewhere in her. Yet she really was almost touched by his insistence on being responsible for such small expenses as they incurred together, which he considered his masculine privilege. It made a pleasant change for her, used as she was to keeping a sharply suspicious eye on her acquaintances, when it came to paying.

But Oswald, in his simplicity, never knew why, after he'd bought her some trifle, she would suddenly give him one of her most ravishing smiles. She had a certain pure, wistful smile, very young, tender and almost virginal, that he could have worshipped. It was, of course, totally misleading.

For him the whole affair was deadly serious, the great romance of his life, for which he'd been waiting and keeping himself, all the more poignant because of the time factor. He wanted to marry her before he rejoined his regiment, and, in the first rapture, actually believed she might consent – she was always so friendly and natural with him; obviously she must like him. But she would never let him propose, implying that marriage was out of the question.

When at last he persisted, and would be put off no longer, she wore her little-girl expression gone wan and sad, whispering that there had been a marriage, which had ended in some unmentionable catastrophe. Her voice shook, and her face, which was always pale, appeared to grow whiter. He saw that she was trembling, and his heart contracted in love and pity. How could he, after this, hurt her by suggesting that they should marry? She had silenced him most effectively, and, it seemed, for good.

She gave him no further confidences; and for a while he was satisfied with knowing that the husband had been somehow eliminated. But he'd told her his whole life story – it was short enough, heaven knows – and, when it dawned on him that, but for the one fact, he knew literally nothing about her, he became vaguely troubled. Could it be that she didn't trust him, or what?

As the days passed, each one a relentless step on the road to parting, tension was growing in him. His rosy dream of a hurried marriage had given place to the more modest aim of getting her consent to a definite engagement before he sailed. But what could he do, now the whole subject was banned?

The very existence of the ban seemed to prove that he didn't love her enough. Yet he adored her, absolutely. Though all his adoration couldn't bring him any closer to her – in fact, she actually seemed to be getting further away.

Horrified by this admission, he tried to ask her what was wrong; only to find himself inexplicably tongue-tied, unable to speak about personal matters. He couldn't understand it. She'd always seemed the easiest person to talk to, formerly he'd poured out all his inmost thoughts to her. Why should constraint now have fallen upon him?

It began to seem as if, after all, there could be no real intimacy between them. Yet, when he rode at her side, she was unchanged, charming and friendly as always, apparently quite happy to be alone with him all day on the moor. Only when he tried to put his troubled thoughts into words she seemed to float away from him, out of his reach.

Of course he took all the blame himself; it must be his fault that, though he would gladly have died for her, he couldn't cross the space which divided them. Some of the suppressed inferiority he'd felt in the army came back to him: his secret fear that his comrades would look down on him – quick, clever, complex people, with all the latest ideas – because he came from this small out-of-the-way country, where life was slow and old-fashioned. Now, with Rejane, it was all far worse.

She tolerated him, out of her kindness of heart. But how dull and stupid he must appear, how provincial, compared with her brilliant friends. No wonder she was impatient with him at times. She'd lately developed a trick, when he looked at her in his dumb bewilderment, imploring her to be kind, of returning the look out of eyes so flatly uncommunicative and disconnected that he felt rebuffed – pushed still further away.

A sort of panic came over him at the thought of the days flying past, bringing them closer to parting. Very soon she would vanish out of his life. But she was everything to him – he couldn't exist without her. Yet, now that the fatal date was in sight, he gave up even trying to approach her, afraid of that blank, repulsing look, and of losing the little intimacy there was between them. At the same time, he despised himself for this defeatist attitude in so all-important a matter. He seemed to have admitted failure in advance, which was contrary to all his instincts and training.

None of this, however, affected Rejane, since outwardly his conduct never varied. If his gentle courtesy sometimes seemed slightly strained, she didn't have to notice – she could ignore it.

*

She was enjoying herself too much to bother about him. Though deviating somewhat from the original plan, her interlude was being a great success. None of her other pretence-lives had been in the least like this healthy outdoor existence, devoted to nature. In her present simple, active life, she was really enjoying the freedom denied her as a young girl by the conventions of her upbringing.

She had always loved riding, the feeling of being above the crowd that came from being on horseback: and she rode well, casual, graceful and at ease, as in everything. As happened with all her mounts, there was at first a bit of a struggle with Coffee, the pony resenting her absolute domination, which deprived it of some animal independence other masters would not have taken away. But, once it submitted, it became almost slavishly devoted, and would follow and come at her call. Pleased by the triumph of her will, she grew as fond of Coffee as she was ever likely to be of any living creature – considerably fonder of it than she was of Oswald.

She rather disliked human beings, really. In the midst of her usual social existence and her love affairs, she remained alone, fundamentally. But she liked to have Oswald in the background, as long as he didn't obtrude on her. His selfless devotion made him an ideal companion. She knew she was perfectly safe while he was about, and needn't worry about anything – least of all about him. Though she couldn't help feeling somewhat contemptuous, because he treated her with such exquisite gentleness, delicacy, and did the very things she wanted him to do. That little store of contempt she had for him was increasing all the time.

When she thought about him at all, she was still curious. She wondered intermittently what had become of his military assurance: why did he, these days, seem almost obliterated, in spite of his splendid body? His deep-blue eyes now had such a melancholy look, even when he was smiling, that she could hardly fail to be conscious of it.

But she soon forgot about him, absorbed as she was in her own pretending. She had a new vision of herself, which included the pony, seeing herself as some sort of wild moorland being, dark hair flying loose, streaming out in the wind like Coffee's weirdly coloured mane and tail, a kind of centaur, careering about the moor, flinging her head back rather as Coffee did, shaking her cloud of dark, dew-spangled hair, half identified with the animal, and half goddess.

This picture had superseded the prehumans and their spells. Gradually they'd been deposed, Oswald's importance declining with theirs, since he was linked with them. Once, she had listened with rapt attention to the curious lilting voice, quite unlike his ordinary voice and perfectly unselfconscious, in which he recited the old stories; seeing him as one of those heroes of whom he spoke, with something of the stern beauty of a young magician in his eyes. The soft singing voice, not really his voice at all, had seemed to reach her uncannily, like a supernatural echo, over the centuries. But now, with her interlude drawing to a close, the supernatural was losing ground – very soon, this whole northern picture would fade out and be forgotten.

There were reminders all the time from her own world. The lover kept imploring her to return. And other letters arrived with the stamps of many different countries, from people who called themselves friends, and, unlike Oswald, couldn't resist the attraction of all that money. They had to keep in contact with it, so they wrote, asking about her plans for the winter, and where she was hiding herself all this time. These communications had their effect, though she continued to drift on from day to day, making no move but waiting for the imperative impulse to come to her, as she knew it would, when this particular pretence-life had run its course – it always happened so.

In the meantime, with darkness falling earlier and earlier, to get through the long evenings at The Hope Deferred was becoming something of a problem. Along the coast was a picturesque town, half seaport, half holiday resort, to which Oswald sometimes drove her to dine and dance. But these occasions were not very successful, except in depriving him of the last shreds of moorland magic. His appeal was purely an outdoor one. In a crowded room full of dressed-up people, he might have been any fair, handsome young officer home on leave.

Dancing with him, she noticed his unblemished skin, which, at close quarters, had almost the rosiness of a baby's under the tan. And that slightly sinister witch-look came on her face, her lovely large lustrous eyes gleaming with a jeering malice. So this was her magician – this rosy, healthy young man! There was nothing even unusual about him, apart from an odd, chanting voice, and a touch of strangeness, which she now saw as a mere manifestation of northern outlandishness, no longer at all attractive.

When her own world called to her suddenly, as she'd known

it would, loud and clear, she was astounded by her surroundings, looking about as if she'd just woken out of a long sleep. She'd been existing all this time in a tranced euphoria of exercise and fresh air. Now, abruptly, she was awake again, in her proper self, eager to get away from the barbarous north. Her spirit seemed to have gone on ahead already to her own luxurious sphere; exasperating that she had to stay behind, with her body.

She wanted to charter a plane on the spot. As this was impossible, and, hearing that a cruising liner was due at the little port in a day or so, she hurriedly booked a passage and sent a cable to her lover to say she was coming back.

But she didn't tell Oswald until they were out on the moor, having lunch in the sun, which was still almost hot at noon. They sat in a sheltered hollow, a shallow bowl surrounded by sunken rocks against which they could lean. While they ate their hard-boiled eggs and drank coffee out of a thermos, the two ponies, tethered nearby, contentedly nosed and nibbled the fine, feathery, fading grass, the same colour as Coffee's tail. Rejane waited till the meal was over and Oswald was collecting the scraps of eggshell and paper, as he always did, before telling him about her arrangements. She saw the young man start violently, as if she had struck him. He dropped his hands, which fell and hung loosely at his sides, while he stood rigid and silent, his face twisted as if in pain.

What on earth was the matter with him? He'd known all along that they would have to part soon. Gazing at him, watching him stare past her with unseeing eyes, Rejane was slightly irritated by this excessive reaction.

To Oswald, who had for some time been in a state of suppressed nervous tension, her announcement came as the final blow. His dream vanished abruptly. Suddenly all his old unpleasant feelings came back – the loneliness and the grievance and the being left out. Now everything was going to be just the same as before. The great love he'd identified with his dream-radiance had failed him. Rejane had failed him. He had adored her. And she'd just made his love ridiculous. He couldn't have explained what he meant by this – his ideas were all confused. He knew only that he felt badly let down.

A devastating sadness overwhelmed him, made more unbearable by his surroundings. That he should have to suffer like this, here, on his beloved moor, struck him as a horrid refinement of torture. How far away already seemed the first happy days when he had displayed its beauties . . . far away and belonging to a time already dead. It now seemed to him that those early days of happiness had led inevitably to his present sorrow; which would in its turn bring him to a still darker state.

*

Rejane was growing increasingly impatient with his silence and gloom. She was sorry now she'd told him she was going. She'd done so only because it seemed unkind to spring her departure on him at the last moment, which confirmed her conviction that kindness was usually a mistake. She should simply have packed up and gone, without giving him any warning.

Now, if she wasn't careful, he would insist on making a tragedy out of his own feelings, which would spoil everything for her. She couldn't stand other people's emotions, and had no intention of putting up with the gloom Oswald was radiating, like a cold fog. Her interlude had been such a success so far that she was determined it shouldn't end in his stupid depression – she must get him out of it somehow. . . . Suddenly standing up, she went to him, and, with a gesture surprisingly spontaneous and natural, took his limp hand in hers, thinking as she did so what a good actress she would have made.

The unexpectedness of this broke through the isolating walls of his misery. So thoroughly was he convinced that she was out of reach, physically most of all, that astonishment overcame all his other feelings. Incredulously he looked down at her slim, by no means incapable, hand, holding his own. Her face was hidden, she stood beside him as if hiding behind her dark hair, whispering shyly, in her little-girl voice, words he could barely catch. He mustn't rush her . . . she hadn't forbidden him to hope . . . seemed to be what she was saying.

Without stopping to consider whether he was justified in taking her seriously, he at once clutched at this unreliable straw she had thrown him. Perhaps, when he came home next time. . . ?

She didn't answer immediately; and, a faint doubt creeping into his mind, he imploringly asked, 'May I kiss you – just this once?' – surely he could believe her if she said yes. 'Do you mind?'

She did mind, in that part of her that always had to remain inviolable and aloof, in perpetual opposition to the other urge that made her deliberately go on attracting men, taking new lovers. But, seeing that it was necessary, she murmured consent, hiding behind her hair, keeping up the pretence of shyness, and consoling herself with the thought that, long before the army disgorged him again, she would have forgotten his existence. Already he seemed a little unreal, almost a dream figure, so soon to be left behind, with his world, for ever. It was like being kissed by a ghost.

The kiss, which Oswald had hoped would confirm his trust, affected him in a way as disturbing as it was unexpected. In the midst of his reverence, he was seized by a passionate impulse; immediately afterwards experiencing a sort of revulsion, reminded of those hated dancing partners of the past. At the same time, an outrageous, though not apparently unfamiliar, thought slid, snakelike, through his head. Some part of him seemed to know already that Rejane despised his restraint and that, if he'd made love to her weeks ago, she would have surrendered – that indeed she'd expected this. But he'd never admitted to knowing it consciously, and would not admit it now, telling himself that the idea was not in accordance with the facts. She'd always kept aloof from him, distant and virginal – it was monstrous to think of her as being like those over-sexed women out East who had tried to seduce him. And yet that strange revulsion he'd felt as he kissed her. . . .

Appalled and confused, he refused to think any further, but stooped to finish his interrupted task.

Since he still remained silent and preoccupied, Rejane looked around for a new distraction. Her eyes fell on the ponies, placidly waiting near; and, in another of her inspired flashes, she asked what would become of Coffee after she'd gone.

She couldn't have chosen a better diversion, for the man was as fond of horses as he was experienced with them. But, before he had time to answer, a dramatic picture appeared in her imagination, and she announced that Coffee must be set free to return to the moors.

This time she could congratulate herself on having got him out of his black mood, so that her interlude could continue peacefully to its conclusion, for his interest was really aroused.

He'd already considered the matter, knowing he would be left with the animal on his hands, and had decided that Coffee should stay at his home, where there were stables and paddocks unused since his father's time. Now he forgot his troubled preoccupations, trying to explain that, once a pony had been trained and ridden, it couldn't go back happily to its wild state; that it wouldn't know how to forage for itself, and would be ostracized by its former companions, because it bore the smell of servitude, which they hated.

Needless to say, he was wasting his time; Rejane refused to listen. In her head was the romantic picture of Coffee flying off to the wilds, free as air – nothing could change it. Oswald didn't want to oppose her, and felt unequal even to the attempt. It occurred to him that Coffee would probably be forgotten, anyhow, in the excitement of her departure.

*

Superficially, calm and friendliness were restored. But neither of them had much to say, and, by mutual consent, they started back to The Hope Deferred earlier than they usually did.

To Rejane the moors were already unreal, outside the reality of her own world. The great pale waste, its purple and gold extinguished, looked phantasmal to her, huge and lonely, with the hummocks of distant tors hunched on the horizon. She'd had more than enough of it, and didn't want to look.

However, the ponies having plodded and scrambled up a long rise, she was confronted by the steep slope down to the valley, floating below in the last luminous light of the sunset, with its farms in their trees, water flashing bright in the folds of the moor beyond. The little lost valley caught her eye for a moment with its gemlike delicacy and brilliant clearness, in miniature there. It had the fragile look of something about to vanish, the almost-bare trees ghostly looking in their few yellow leaves. At ground level, dusk was already thickening, while the treetops still shimmered ghostlike in sunset gold. Suddenly, as she looked, the valley sank out of sight, all its toylike brightness put out as the sun disappeared and the lumpish tors heaved themselves up all round it in startling significance, huge and uncanny, the gloomy dark masses of moorland standing out menacingly.

Suddenly then, at this first moment after the sun had set, she shivered, feeling frost in the air. The cold seemed to leap upon her like some wild animal. She had a brief moment of superstitious fear, feeling for the first time the power of the hostile north, feeling this country as her enemy – she wouldn't be really safe from it until she was on the ship. Her one desire now was to get away. She had a positive craving for the noise and bustle of cities after the silence and emptiness of the north – if only she could be gone, and all this left far behind and forgotten!

Now up came Oswald to ride at her side, a bit subdued, but protective as ever in his knight-errant way, to guard her from her own superstitious fears. Odd how he always seemed to sense what she was feeling.

'Chilly?' He now put out a comforting, helpful hand, to turn up her coat collar. Then, evidently thinking that conversation was called for, he began telling her about the ancient castle fortress of Bannenberg, to which the old half-legendary kings were supposed to have gone, after receiving magical warning of their approaching end. An echo of his musical lilt could be heard; but his brilliant eyes brooded over her, filled with melancholy and misgiving. She got the impression that he was talking to reassure himself almost as much as her.

And, being sensitized just then, whether she liked it or not, to northern influences, she had an instantaneous impersonal vision of him as a man born to a certain tradition of nobility and honourable service, now lost to the world. Finding no one and nothing to serve with the nobility in him, he was rejected, left isolated and unfulfilled. He'd dedicated his knightly service to her; that was why his need for contact with her was so urgent. It was more than being in love with her – something more compelling. His life, almost, depended on loving her. She alone could save him from being rejected, cast out.

All this she saw in an instantaneous flash, as if from outside herself, immediately afterwards thinking, from *inside*. Why couldn't he save himself? Why should he expect *her* to save him? It seemed presumptuous, as if he were making use of her as a means to an end. At the same time, she was gratified because at last she possessed his secret; which meant that the man himself was no longer in the least interesting – anyhow, she'd finished with him already as she had with everything here. She was about to send Coffee cantering on, leaving Oswald behind, when she changed her mind, and continued to ride beside him.

She'd never been to Bannenberg, or wanted to go, always avoiding the places that tourists went to. But now she suddenly said she must see the final resting-place of the old kings before she left the country – it would make a suitable expedition for her last day here.

Oswald had already planned in his head a sentimental tour of their favourite places, hoping they might have a softening effect at the end, and at once started protesting. Bannenberg was much too far for the ponies; even by car they could only just get there and back in one day. And wouldn't she have a lot to do then? Surely she wouldn't want to spend the whole day in the car? What about her packing?

No longer susceptible to the north or its influences, she cared nothing for the horrible country, simply regarding it with extreme repugnance. But she had her reasons for wanting to go on this trip, and was quite determined.

They came down to the little cluster of dwellings, which seemed huddled together as if for warmth in the dismal twilight. And, the whole length of the village street, Oswald continued his argument: it was too late in the season for Bannenberg, which could be approached only by a lonely coast road, liable at this time of the equinoctial gales to be swept by high tides and rendered impassable. Only a year ago a section of the cliff had collapsed, and with it part of the castle, carried away by the rough seas that incessantly battered the wild, exposed coastline.

Rejane was hardly listening, he hardly seemed real. Only, occasionally, in the dusk, her eye caught the ghostly white gleam of his hair, falling forward as he leaned towards her, talking with spectral emphasis and persistence; till at last, to her relief, the lights of The Hope Deferred came in sight. Its bright windows looked hospitable and cheerful; it seemed the one point of life and light in all that dreary cold desolation.

With a charming smile for the youth who ran out to take Coffee's bridle, she slid from the saddle and hurried in, into the warm; Oswald, like winter personified with his white head, closely pursuing.

*

Now, under the lights, he could see the inflexible look he'd known all the time must be on her face, against which no words or actions of his could prevail. But, obsessed, he insisted on finding an atlas and showing her Bannenberg, the northernmost headland of his northern country, like a signpost, pointing straight to the Pole.

Holding out her hands to the pile of logs blazing in the wide fireplace, Rejane gave the map a perfunctory glance. And, in spite of the heat of the fire, she suddenly shivered again, as she had on the moor, feeling the hostility of the frozen north, exclaiming, 'Heavens, how cold it is tonight!'

Always obliging, Oswald hastily threw on some more logs without being distracted from his argument. While swarms of sparks fled up the chimney, he told her that the castle was already considered unsafe; tourists were warned that they went there at their own risk – one of these days the whole ancient edifice would sink under the waves, ceaselessly eroding its foundations.

All the more reason, Rejane lightly answered, for her to see it while this was still possible. Her momentary chill forgotten, she stood in the firelight, smiling and adamant, not to be deflected from her purpose, which was no mere whim but a calculated design: by keeping him fully occupied throughout her last day, she would prevent any inconvenient display of emotion.

The young man was confused by the contrast between her outward serenity and good humour, and the emanation he felt of something ruthless opposing him from within her, demolishing each objection he raised, a radiation of implacable will, which crushed all his protests stone dead, finally crushing him too and forcing him to surrender.

As if she'd been waiting just for this, as soon as he'd given in she seemed to withdraw and become inaccessible, already gone from him in spirit. He was aware the whole time that they would have only one more evening together and, paralysed by the thought, it was hard for him to keep up an ordinary conversation. She did nothing to help him. The silences grew longer and longer. Remoteness seemed to gather about her like snow, as though, in the warm room, snow were falling and hiding her from him. The illusion even affected his vision, so that he couldn't see her distinctly.

Unable to bear any more of the coldness and distance that was in the air, although it was still quite early, he got up to go, saying he had a headache, which was the truth. She seemed nowhere near him when he said good-night, her large lustrous eyes looking through him to something else, the smile on her lovely face not for him.

Now he felt he couldn't leave without some sign of recognition. Lingering miserably, he asked her to be ready when he came the next day. They'd have to start early if they were to get back at a reasonable hour.

But she still seemed not there for him, somehow, with an inward, mysterious, smiling look on her face that froze him and sent him home sick at heart.

4

OSWALD felt better when he woke in the morning; most of his blurred impressions of the previous night seemed sheer imagination. Dressing quickly, he left the house before breakfast, and, munching an apple picked up on the way, went out to the car.

His main concern was to elude his mother and sister, who had lately begun to complain of his continual absence, and had already protested against the Bannenberg trip. Last night his headache had come in useful, enabling him to avoid argument by going to bed. Now he could but hope to slip away unobserved.

However, he had no chance to do so before his mother rushed out of the house in her dressing-gown – a distraught, dishevelled figure, pathetic and slightly absurd – imploring him not to go to Bannenberg. She'd had 'a warning' during the night, a dream or a premonition. He could hardly understand what she was saying, as, incoherent with agitation, she came stumbling up to him, tripping over the long dressing-gown.

Oswald frowned disapprovingly. He always discouraged her psychic tendencies, both because he considered them undignified and because they reminded him of certain imaginative traits he'd inherited which were unsuited to a cavalryman. As a rule, she was easily crushed. Now, by ignoring his severity, as he steered her back into the house, she forced him to realize how strong her conviction of coming disaster must be. He couldn't possibly leave her in this state. Common humanity required him to stay with her, at least for a few minutes, especially after the way he'd been neglecting her lately.

Feeling exasperated and victimized, he tried to calm her by saying he was far too experienced a driver to get into difficulties, whatever the road was like. But her fears were of a less concrete nature, she refused to be pacified, continuing to pour out a flood of confused pleading and protest; which he didn't even attempt to understand now, merely uttering random reassurances at intervals.

In the course of these futile exchanges, time was slipping past. He saw that he would inevitably be late in getting to the hotel; and the idea of Rejane waiting for him, doubtless becoming indignant because he didn't turn up, drove him nearly frantic. Unconsciously he fixed his eyes on the door; and his mother, noticing this, suddenly clutched his sleeve, as if afraid he might make a dash for it.

At her touch, his extreme impatience turned into anger: he almost hated her for delaying him with this absurd rigmarole. And where was Vera? Why didn't she come to his rescue?

As if answering him, his sister hurried into the room, glanced nervously from one of them to the other, and stopped just inside the door.

'I *must* go, Mother.' Oswald shook off the hand clutching his arm, strode across to the door, and, as he passed Vera, muttered furiously, 'Why can't you look after her properly? It's your job.'

A kind of hiatus ensued in his mind, he seemed to gape incredulously at the sound of his own angry voice. Never before in his life had he spoken to any woman in that enraged brutal tone. It was horrifying that his mother and sister should be the first to hear it. Appalled by his own behaviour, he thought, Nobody would be likely to call me The Parson now, wondering what had become of his former gentleness and consideration.

He raced all the way to the hotel, to find Rejane, as he'd expected, in a very bad temper because, after asking her specially to be ready, he'd kept her waiting so long. She wouldn't listen to his apologies or explanations, forcing him to endure her reproaches, as he'd endured his mother's, as they started off on the long trip, which seemed to him to have begun under the worst possible auspices.

*

Though he sat bolt upright behind the wheel, the athletic young man gave the impression of supporting with difficulty some tremendous weight. Vaguely, he supposed it was knowing he must sustain the effort of driving fast the whole way on this bad road which was oppressing him, like his headache of the previous evening, though less as a physical pain than an obscure sort of unease at the back of his thoughts.

Even when Rejane recovered her usual good humour, which she soon did, sulking not being one of her faults, Oswald couldn't throw off this weight of uneasiness, which made it hard for him to respond. Her smiles were, in fact, rather painful to him. How could she be so gay when tomorrow they had to part? They stopped to eat their picnic lunch by the roadside; and he couldn't help thinking that she looked heartless, basking there in the sun, her fur coat thrown back, calmly eating a devilled egg. Though she didn't want to move, he refused to linger, and, as soon as they'd finished, insisted on setting off again, aware all the time of the miles still to be driven.

Helplessly, he felt her displeasure. He could do nothing about it. He knew he was a dull companion but found nothing to say, overwhelmed by an accumulation of pressures. He couldn't get rid of the feeling of having too much to carry – the entire responsibility for the trip as well as his distress over their coming separation, his guilt feeling about his mother, and the unacknowledged effect of her superstitious fears.

Clouds appeared, quickly covering the sky. It became evident to him that, before the end of the day, there would be a storm. What infernal luck that the weather should change exactly now. He was seized by a violent sense of the injustice of life, the hostility of the whole world. He'd always tried all his life to do what was right and fair, yet even the weather now had to add to his difficulties. It was too much. All at once, war seemed to have been declared between him and the entire world, where everything was leagued against him.

The cliff road could be really dangerous in a storm – they ought to go back. But to say so would make Rejane only more determined to go on. It was no use arguing, she would always defeat him. Glancing at her face, he seemed to detect there signs of self-will not noticed before.

With sudden horror, he realized that he was including her with the alien hostile world, organized against him. And the idea already seemed to have destroyed his former uncritical respect and love, so that he continued, half against his will, to identify her with the general hostility that was piling up great fire-edged fortresses of cloud in the sky. His face grew more and more sombre as he drove on, in almost complete silence, in the slowly darkening light, which gradually assumed a coppery tinge, ominous-seeming after the weeks of sunshine.

*

Since the last little grim stony village they'd passed not a house, not a soul. There was only the everlasting grey moor with its lumpish tors stretching in every direction, an occasional sunbeam pointing a long, thin finger at it, ending in a spotlight of lurid brilliance. Or, from time to time, several rays would pierce the dense cloud, emerging like fansticks from one point, or coming from different parts of the sky to pass stealthily to and fro like the stilt-legs of luminous giants whose heads were hidden above the sky. Now, belts of forest began to alternate with the moorland, black, bristling firwoods and dense huddles of bare, deciduous trees that seemed to be strangling each other, drowning in their own debris of dead leaves and entanglements of smashed limbs.

Rejane stared out at all this in silence, bored and disdainful, till a sudden nerve-shattering clatter of loose stones flying up made her comment indignantly on the state of the road.

'What else can you expect?' Back came Oswald's muted musical melancholic voice. 'It's only made up once a year for the summer tourists. Nobody comes in the winter. There won't be another car along here till next spring.'

'We'll actually be the last people to come this year?'

For some reason her original sense of northern strangeness revived at this thought and she gave him a wondering glance, which he, occupied with avoiding the ruts and potholes, failed to observe. It was all so uncivilized, so alien, so inexpressibly strange, to her: and Oswald himself was so much a part of the strangeness. His wintry blue eyes were related to the desolate landscape, filled with the weird mystic gloom she imagined as the gloom of the endless winters, when the sun went stooping across the sky, following its low arc, like a runner who must not be seen, mysteriously diffusing its tender rose through the falling snow – unexpectedly the spell of the north worked again.

Suddenly she was startled by a tremendous snapping and crackling under the wheels, as they crushed a tangle of branches blown down into the road. And now, all at once, winter seemed very near, waiting, just out of sight, like a threat in the air. Just for a second she felt a childish fear that winter would overtake her before she could get away – that she'd be caught and held her against her will in the hostile, alien north. It lasted only the barest moment; just long enough for her to recall the headland she'd seen on the map, pointing straight to the Pole, and to wish she hadn't insisted on this expedition. Last night Oswald had been desperately anxious to dissuade her from coming – why didn't he now suggest turning back? Before, he'd always been so quick to catch her mood and fulfil her least wish, almost before she herself had become aware of it.

Glancing at his set profile, she had the idea he kept silent now out of spite, trying to force her to say she'd had enough – which, of course, she never would. Indignantly she turned away, to look out of the window again; only to be flung against him as the car lurched, skidding wildly on what seemed the loose stones of a river-bed, rushing the steep bank on the other side. She opened her mouth in exasperated complaint. But, before she could get a word out, they reached the top, and her breath was snatched away by the wind that came charging at them, straight off the open sea.

She could only grasp, everything else forgotten, astonished by the sight of this vast, heaving mass of angry-looking water, appearing so unexpectedly, right under her nose. The road ran along the very edge of the cliff; there was nothing at all in front of her but the ocean of foam-capped rollers, dotted with rocky islets, each in its collar of foam – indomitable, even though drowned, the moorland tors kept their heads above water. Coloured like anthracite far out, the sea changed nearer the shore to peculiar acid shades of yellow and green, the waves rearing up, racing landwards, like the arched necks of horses, their wild white manes blowing back. The road was high above them most of the time. But periodically the cliff subsided, they sank to sea-level and drove on the hard white sand of the beaches which interspersed the jagged, stark, brutal rocks, where the waves towered high above *them*. Most extraordinary, it seemed to Rejane, to be looking *up* at those huge greengage-coloured monsters, pounding in like wild horses, crashing down their hoofs on the rocks with a noise like thunder, filling the air with their savage neighing and the misty fume of their breath. All her bored apprehension was blown away instantly, and replaced by exhilaration.

The waves exploded in tremendous thunder, the wind slammed and banged and battered the car, as if trying to blow it into the sea or smash it to smithereens on the rocks. While, like some magic snowstorm, thickening the misted air, pale sea-birds of many varieties rose and fell, or hung almost motionless on barely quivering wings, their fierce-looking beaks opening and shutting in ghostly screams, no sound of which pierced the louder tumult of wind and water.

All this she found most exciting after the dreary, desolate monotony of the moor. This tumultuous wildness of the elements appealed to her witch-self. Unaware of the cold, she let down her window to feel the salty wind on her skin; and now caught a thin, eerie thread of sound woven into the turmoil, a high, unearthly screeching from the crowd of escorting birds, drifting along with them effortlessly, as if drawn by the draught of the car. Listening entranced to this uncanny other-world accompaniment to the sea's vociferous clamour and the bellowing of the wind, she forgot Oswald's existence. She'd already left him in spirit, and didn't even attempt to hide her rapt demonic expression – the man saw it, and was aghast.

*

Her lovely face, in its luminous pure pallor, with all its planes and outlines emphasized by the wind, the hair flowing back from it like dark water, had a pure unearthliness, like the face of a water-maiden, an ethereal quality the heavy, clodlike earth and its clod-hopping inhabitants could never know. But it also had the inhuman smile of a water-*witch*, chilling his blood, as if the woman he loved had revealed herself as this lovely but soulless and evil *thing*.

He shivered, in spite of his thick overcoat, not only because of the cold, though he felt it after his years near the equator, and had meant to ask her to shut the window. He left the words unspoken now, silenced by his glimpse of that undisguised demon-look, which chilled him to the bone.

It was the unawareness of her rapt face that was most hurtful and insulting to him, showing so clearly her obliviousness of him, her indifference to him and to their coming separation. He remembered how she'd told him he could hope, and was forced to acknowledge openly what he already suspected in secret – that she'd said it only to keep him quiet.

Suddenly he was stung into acute resentment. What a fool she must have thought him. How she must have been laughing at him all the time, sneering at his credulity, his innocence. He was ashamed – his love had been degraded into something shameful, something he wanted to throw away. He looked at her again, intentionally filling his eyes with her cruel indifference. So she really was part of the general conspiracy against him. He hadn't quite believed it before; now he let the idea take possession of him. He couldn't endure his love any longer – he must get rid of it somehow. So he kept glancing at her, whenever he could take his eyes off the road, as if her heartless nonchalance, at which he'd been unable to look a minute ago, had become a magnet, irresistibly attracting his eyes.

But nothing was clear in his head. All his feelings and thoughts were confused by a stony sort of despair, which threw everything out of focus and made him feel hopeless and almost dazed. Curving continually, never leaving the sea, the road closely followed the indentations of the rugged coastline, always enveloped in the salt spray of the breakers blowing inland, with which his obscured ideas seemed to mingle. He couldn't tell where the confusion in his head ended and the haze outside began, he drove by instinct only, in the metallic light of the storm he was racing, pressing his foot on the accelerator, taking the dangerous curves much too fast, and hearing, above all the confused, tumultuous weather noises, the tiny chatter of stones showering over the edge of the cliff, as the wheels spun dizzily, almost over.

He wasn't exactly taking the risk on purpose. His vague impression was that centrifugal force carried the car too far out, and that his curious daze prevented him from correcting the swing until the last possible moment, with the help of the wind. If, at the next bend, the wind failed to catch the car's body and throw it back, by himself he wouldn't be able to check the tendency outwards and over the edge. . . . He came suddenly upon this thought, as if unawares, and it roused him briefly, an outrage to his whole nature as well as his disciplined training. He felt for a moment as though he must be drunk or delirious. He wanted to stop the car, get out and walk about until he'd recovered.

But down came the weight of pressure on him, there was no time to stop, he had to keep going. The situation had got beyond him, beyond his control, so he left the driving to a kind of mechanical intelligence and lapsed into a queer, indeterminate state, in which he felt cut off from his own consciousness, altogether separate from his normal self, as if dreaming.

His eyes gazed out, not really seeing. But when the old castle fortress appeared ahead, and he pointed it out to Rejane, he seemed to come back a little towards himself, feeling that he'd been detailed for some operation beyond his endurance, which nevertheless must be endured and brought to a successful conclusion. He could only rely on the years of self-imposed discipline to see him through. He was still in that darkened confused state; his real consciousness still remained somewhere apart, and dissociated.

*

Rejane could hardly distinguish between the place they'd come to see and the rocky promontory of which it was part. Medieval incantations seemed to have conjured it from the cliff. She had to tilt her head far back before she saw, among the fantastic cloud fortifications of the approaching storm, the no less fantastic battlements hewn by men, with primitive implements and indomitable will, out of the living rock. The grim old place looked impregnable and undamaged, until they came nearer and saw a black gaping mouth where the structure fell in a frozen cascade of stone, down into the waves, which came charging over the debris, leaping up savagely at those fragments that hung suspended and out of reach, petrified in the act of their mass-suicidal plunge into the wild water.

The car passed over a narrow drawbridge and stopped; and Rejane stepped out on to a platform of flat grey rock like a natural forecourt. Already in an exalted mood, lifted above herself, she ignored an instantaneous impression of danger, which repeated the warning she'd previously received from this hostile country. Now it was repeated much more emphatically, though with no more result, by the wind, which swooped down upon her, viciously tearing at her hair and clothes, trying to sweep her off her feet; while the sea, with a ferocious roar, in which barbaric battle-cries seemed to mingle, hurled itself at her, hundreds of tons of solid water shattering on the rocky foundations of the place, shaking it, flinging up sheets of spray high above her head. Booming and bellowing, the wave rushed on through the dungeons and drowned cavern-like chambers under her feet, before it withdrew, hissing like a million serpents, to meet the oncoming roar of the next explosion.

Instead of warning her, this combined onslaught of wind and sea merely increased her exhilaration. She gave the sea a half-smiling look of triumph, as if it really had tried, and failed, to carry her off; and, made audacious by her imagined victory, she at once resolved to break into the stronghold itself. She would force it to give up its secrets, revive, by the power of her imagination, the grisly dramas once played out there. She had heard how a ghostly messenger warned the old kings who were about to die; who then retired to this remote peninsula near the northern cap of the world, where the last rites were performed – the ghoulish sacrifices and blood spells which, even in those barbaric times, were too infamous to be known; they had always to be kept secret.

The whole place had a curious horror fascination for her, shut away here in this awful desolation, close to the deathly white frozen Pole. Living so much in imaginary melodramas, she now felt an urge to identify herself with the murderous spells of the dim past and the blood-smeared primitive magic of those dead wolfish men, as if, like one of the great snakes, she could ingurgitate their powers into her own being. It was the same fascination of evil – of the mysterious *northern* evil – that had first attracted her to the tors.

Most strangely now, just when the spell of the north had seemed extinct, it again enthralled her. The mysterious, dangerous effluence she'd originally found so alluring seemed deliberately to have brought her here to its climax, which only Bannenberg could bring forth. She looked up at the great rugged mass of stone, closed and secretive, its tremendous doors, iron-studded, impossible to open. But they must open for her. Suddenly she remembered Oswald and looked around for him – he was peering into the entrails of the car, just behind her.

'How can we get in?' she demanded peremptorily, impatient because he hadn't opened the way already – what else was he there for?

He straightened up, letting the cover fall. Its metallic clang was lost in the thunderous crash of another wave, fountains of spray burst up, from which Rejane had to jump forward, nearer to him. His deep-blue eyes stared with a peculiar blank brilliance in the grey thunder light, gazing at her with a strange fixity, which she didn't notice.

'There's nothing to see inside. Let's go back before the storm.' His voice had a queer flat sound of reasonableness, perhaps not entirely sane.

'But I want to go in.'

Not quite sane either in her obstinacy, she overrode reason, arrogantly asserting her will over his, refusing to tolerate even the least opposition. At the moment she looked upon him as a sort of tool, existing solely for the purpose of opening the door for her – a role which he, with strange, mad passivity, accepted as if there were no alternative in all creation.

It seemed nothing to do with him, really. Detached, like a robot, he went, without wasting any more time or words, to a side door she hadn't noticed, and, after struggling with it, got it open so that she could pass.

Dropping him from her thoughts as though he had ceased to be, Rejane went in, not even noticing whether he followed or stayed outside, as she stepped into what at first seemed total darkness.

Her eyes quickly became accommodated to such light as entered where the roof had caved in, and she saw that windows were non-existent. There were only narrow slits through which arrows could pass. It was a really frightening place in the near-darkness. Untold atrocities, perpetrated in the distant past, had left a legacy of abomination all the intervening years had been unable to obliterate. An aura of sadism and terror clung to the walls, much as shreds of threadbare fabric clung to the doorless archways. The walls themselves were damp and clammy to the touch, always sweating from the salt spume: and the paving-stones too had a slimy surface, uneven, broken or missing, so that to take a step in any direction was dangerous.

If not the actual danger, then that worse thing, the exudation of ancient evil, would have sent most people hurrying out into the light of day. To Rejane, however, the malevolence in the air was the appropriate atmosphere of the past, already starting to come alive again for her. The magic of the north demonstrated its power by reclaiming her in this way from the civilized world, which, until such a short time ago, had been her only reality. The world of cities was obliterated again by the other more potent, more ancient spell, here about to be consummated. Entranced, she gave herself up as to an unseen presence leading her on, moving with curious sleep-walking sureness, unperturbed by the many pitfalls through which she might have been precipitated into the submerged torture chambers and oubliettes lower down, or by the awful cold blight that was in the atmosphere.

Spellbound, she had become a queen in her dreaming, crowned, feeling the weight of trailing velvet, ermine white at her wrists and throat, as she approached the inner funerary chamber, the core of the place, for which, unconsciously, she was making. A flurry of misshapen ghosts greeted her entrance, shooting up to the groined ceiling, and crouching down, gnome-like, in the folds of the arras – for an instant she saw it all quite distinctly: the sable, gold-emblazoned hangings of the catafalque, lit by many tall candles, which, guttering in the draught of her trailing robes, sent flying in all directions the shadows of the fierce, bearded men standing with drawn swords, on guard.

Then, abruptly, her fantasy fled, swift as the shadows. Water sounds, which it had reduced to the droning of incantations, rose suddenly to a loud imperious shouting. All of a sudden the sea sounded frighteningly near.

She had gone so far in her dream that it took her another second to come back. To her amazement and horror, she saw then, in the daylight that entered as if through the mouth of a cave, a shocking precipice, right at her feet, where the floor collapsed into the seething water – from out there came the ominous rumbling boom of an approaching wave.

And, before she had time to think even, a terrifying great wall of water was rushing at her, bearing down upon her like an avalanche, yelling triumphantly as it came, and gurgling with sadistic glee. Her heart plunged in sudden terror, instinctively she jumped back, and felt a sickening movement beneath her, as the stone rocked under her weight, covered with slippery weed on which she could get no foothold. Wildly swaying, she struggled and struggled to get her balance, while the mountainous surge of water raced towards her, a ghostly, pale, impossible bird floating above, its reflected wings writhing like snakes on the monstrously swollen bulk of grey water.

With the ghastly sickness of nightmare she struggled in vain, her hands helplessly clutching and clawing the bare, slimy walls, finding nothing to grip, the rock always tilting further under her feet, and the wave towering up hideously, filling the world with its hugeness, its crashing thunder and icy cold flying spray.

In a blind, unconscious frenzy she bent herself back until

her spine seemed to break; hearing, above all that insane water noise her own short, horrible, unnatural scream; seeing, at this moment of ultimate horror, the pitiless, pale bird-eye indifferently watching; as, in an agonized slither, she started lurching, sliding and slipping, helpless, down to the sea. With an icy shock as though death had already claimed her, she felt the cold spray on her face.

Instantly then, another shock shook right through her, she felt herself grasped and dragged back. A pair of arms went round her like iron bands, holding her, pulling her back somehow, away from the charging mountain of water and its fatal, freezing breath. She was barely conscious, shuddering so convulsively that she was almost sick. But the arms remained locked round her, and, gradually, she was dragged back, limply sliding and hardly conscious, over the unsteady stones: until the floor became solid again, the daylight dimmed; the sea's thunder receded, there was no more impossible great floating bird-ghost.

*

Rejane felt the floor steady under her feet, heard the sea noise much diminished, and slowly began to understand she was safe. But she could not easily return to the living world. She had died, her life had been violated by the death-kiss of the sea. She was still shuddering so horribly from the shock, which had shaken her to the very last fibre, that the solid stone too seemed to be shaking round her, as if the whole place were about to come down.

How could she believe she'd escaped from the sea, when she still heard the waves thudding against the stone, shaking the ruin with their explosions? She seemed to see all the time that awful great gap tearing her dream of the past, the horrible wall of water charging at her, the spectral, snake-winged bird with its fierce, evil, slashing beak. She could not come back to life while she saw these things, she could not speak or stop shivering.

She still belonged to that ghastly unstable world where there was nothing to hold to, everything swirling round her, the rock slipping under her feet. Only if she could make the moment of her slithering, sickening plunge seem unreal, would she be able to return to her own existence. This knowledge came, not from her shocked, non-functioning brain, but from a far deeper instinctual source, productive only of absolute certainties.

Without *almost* believing that she was a superior being, she could not live. So she couldn't allow herself to know she had looked in the eye of extinction, or felt the sea's icy kiss. She must convince herself that this had not happened, and she must do it *now* – unless, in these first few moments after the event, she could isolate it, cut it off from her consciousness, she was done for; she wouldn't be able to go on living at all.

With all the power of her will, she set about trying to transform the memory of what had just happened into fearful but absurd nightmare that couldn't possibly have been real; struggling as desperately now with her will as her body had struggled then to obliterate all but a confused dreamlike impression, as of something imaginary. She didn't know whether she would ever be able to do it. She was still so cold, shivering, freezing cold, everything wavering round her. The iron grip holding her seemed the one stable point in the universe.

Suddenly, then, she became aware of Oswald, who had saved her and was still holding her in his encircling arms, through which she could feel pulsing, like an electric current, the vibration of his desire. And, like a reflex, at this first instant of recognition, the part of her that always resented a man's touch stiffened, and she heard her unsteady voice say, 'Let me go. . . . ' Although, as she realized immediately afterwards, this was the very last thing she really wanted. She was really in desperate need of him at that moment. Alone, she couldn't recover from her terrifying experience. She needed the help of another person to overcome it and re-establish her in her life. The warmth of a living body was needed to counteract that other coldly inhuman touch. She needed to be identified with the life force throbbing in Oswald's passion in order to prove that she was also alive and a part of life.

In spite of her protest, Oswald was what she needed, and Oswald she must have. Let him take her and warm her back to her life – let him exorcize the spell of the sea. His arms around her were hard and unyielding like bonds, but they were burning, pulsing with the urgency of his passion, to which she gave herself up, relaxing thankfully in their ungentle grasp.

*

It was to escape the load of his responsibilities and unhappiness, of which he was aware only as an undefined threat or weight, that the young man had followed her into the ruined castle. Inside, his blank state intensified by the dark and the sleep-walking motions of his companion, he'd drifted after her without a thought, as though being pulled by a magnet.

His action in catching her when she fell had been mechanical, purely. But the effort involved had brought him partially out of his daze, to which he now wished to return.

Why was he here in this horrible, dungeonlike place? Suddenly becoming more objectively conscious of Rejane, he remembered that she'd forced him to come, resenting this almost as much as he resented the pressure of her body, forcing him to be aware of the physical, when he wanted to exist only in the abstract. He wanted nothing to do with her, so why was she still in his arms?

Seeing her leaning against him, limp and trembling and almost unconscious, incapable, obviously, of standing alone, in a sort of panic-resentment, he dragged her a few steps nearer the door. But he gave up the attempt at once. He'd never be able to get her outside, to drag her along all those black tunnels he vaguely recalled.

Panic subsiding, he felt a remote surprise at the change in his own feelings. It was such a short time, hours rather than days, since to be holding her in his arms would have seemed like heaven. In this short time she'd become a stranger to him, a woman he neither knew nor wanted to know – least of all in the carnal sense. What could have put that thought into his head? The very notion of sensuality at such a time was repulsive to him.

This was the moment when he felt Rejane's slight stiffening and heard her voice murmur unsteadily, 'Let me go. . . .'

An instantaneous flash went through him, like the lurid flashes and sparks from an electric train. 'No – why should I?' he said; or rather, his voice said it for him, in the brutal, embittered tone his mother and sister had been the first to hear. All the resentment he had accumulated during his whole life seemed released now, as by a breaking dam, in this violent electric discharge, directed against the unjust world in general, and Rejane in particular, who had destroyed his dream and debased the love that should have been pure and perfect.

It was as though, during his dazed absence from himself, the evil influences of the place had taken possession of him, filling him with a sort of madness The Parson could never have known. A strong, savage excitement was working in him, unmistakably pleasurable, though it was perverse and sadistic – The Parson could never have harboured any such cruel sensation.

Some small remnant of his everyday self was disgusted and shocked; but this was immediately submerged by a new self which, in cynical rebellion against The Parson and all his works, swept his ideals into the dustbin as so much rubbish. To hell with The Parson!

Now he was going to take what he wanted. The sinister flash again, as the knowledge of his intention exploded into his nerves and blood. Now he was going to take his revenge.

The fierce excitement went on raging through him, while, with a sensation of something malign breaking out, full of destructive power, he clasped Rejane tightly to him and crushed his lips down on hers. At this moment he derived a peculiar satisfaction from knowing that he was outraging his most fundamental beliefs by performing an illicit cruel act, abhorrent to everybody. The sadism that had replaced his tender love rejoiced at the prospect of humiliating the lovely body he'd hitherto regarded as unattainable and almost holy. Really she was no better than the army wives, on whom he also seemed to be revenging himself by embracing her so fiercely.

Still holding her firmly gripped by one arm, without lifting his mouth from hers, in a single sweeping movement he tore down and flung on the floor an armful of the tattered hangings, rotten and almost transparent with age, which adhered to the wall just behind him.

*

And Rejane, who normally couldn't stand any form of coercion or crudity, actually encouraged his ruthless excitement, because it was almost like the blind destructive force of the sea, and she seemed to be substituting this situation for her other awful ordeal, which was thus rendered harmless. Her thoughts were still all confused; but she felt obscurely that she was making the disaster unreal, by repeating it now in this way, because her ravisher was a mere man who, basically, couldn't harm her.

Oswald's warmth was an instant relief to her trembling body, which had been frozen almost to ice. His ungentle grasp restored stability to the world and anchored her firmly in it; his hard hands pulled her back to life. The violence with which he held her clenched stopped her shivering. The mortal cold melted out of her, and the blood, which had seemed static in her veins, circulated again. As warmth came back to her and her shuddering ceased, what had happened began to seem less and less possible: till presently, just as she wished, all that had taken place since she arrived in the north assumed the aspect of an incoherent dream, culminating in the nightmare just over – that it should have taken the form of the falling nightmares of her childhood confirmed this.

Since each grotesque, incredible detail was a fresh proof that she must be dreaming, she could accept a sadistic lover who, as if with the intention of inflicting pain, crushed her much-cherished body against the rock, which the pile of rags, damp, mildewed, disintegrating, softened no more than a heap of cobwebs.

Her heart was beating fast with triumphant relief – the sea had no more power over her! It had all been a nightmare, simply. Now she listened to the waves with a kind of gloating, as to the cries of a vanquished enemy she humiliated deliberately by this performance of the sexual act – which was the act of life – so soon after her victory, so near to the scene of the struggle.

Safely back in her life, she felt stronger than ever before; herself again, but with this triumph added, that she'd conquered the power of the sea. She could now positively enjoy her sensations, the very strangeness of which stimulated her somewhat cold eroticism.

Lying in Oswald's arms she exulted because danger and death had been put far from her and had no more reality – nor had he, incidentally. All the same, she was glad to have taken him as her lover, which, to her sense of theatre, had always seemed the only appropriate climax and end to their relationship. It was quite true that she despised him rather for making no advances to her – a deficiency he'd corrected at the last moment with the rough violence to be expected of the barbaric north. She didn't hold it against him, complacent and well disposed towards all the world as she could afford to be.

5

OUTSIDE, the storm hadn't broken. They emerged into a world still ominously roofed over by leaden clouds. In this sombre light, glancing at her companion, Rejane was struck by his face of stony despair, most unsuited to her own triumphant feelings – for her, this was a moment for jubilation. In the overflow of her victorious good nature she wanted to cheer him up and asked what was the matter. Getting no answer, she supposed he was downcast because everything was so soon over, and cheerfully said, 'We'd have been frozen if we'd stopped in there any longer. Besides, I thought you were in such a hurry to start back?'

The wind swooped down on her then, she ran to the car, jumped in, slammed the door and pulled the window right up, too anxious to escape the northern elements to notice his continued silence and gloom. Wrapping herself in the rug, she quickly discarded those garments that were uncomfortably damp, snuggled into the luxurious warmth of the fur coat she'd left on the seat, and turned the driving mirror towards her to do her face.

The love she'd always felt for her own beauty was her deepest, most sincere emotion, and for a while she was oblivious of everything but the reflection. She had no thought but the admiring wonder inspired by that lovely face, almost luminous in the dulled light, more radiantly beautiful than she'd ever seen it. Far above the commonplace vulgar world, where no threat could touch her, she floated, entranced by her own magnolia-pale loveliness.

When she came down to earth again, she glanced out rather

disdainfully at Oswald, still brushing and beating his clothes, in a stubborn, unsuccessful attempt to remove the traces of seaweed and water. Why did he fuss over such trifles? She called to him to make haste.

The afternoon had gone bleak and horrible under the protracted threat of the storm. When they finally drove off, it seemed to her that all the viciousness of the coming winter pursued them, pouring out of the ruin behind, as if Bannenberg were its stronghold, the wind blowing great guns. She wanted only to forget the horrible place and didn't even glance back, luxuriating in the warmth of the car, after all she'd been through in there, curling up in her corner with catlike content.

Gradually, however, Oswald's silence became impossible to ignore, obtruding itself upon her self-satisfaction. Persistently striking a discordant note, it forced her, eventually, to look at his face, which seemed to have taken on a greyish tinge under the tan. His fine blue eyes stared out with brilliant fixity, always averted from her; and never a word did he utter – she might not have been there at all.

She was accustomed to very different treatment from her various lovers, and began to feel irritated. His silence got on her nerves. She resented it much more than his sadism just now, which she'd already almost forgotten, remembering only enough of his recent behaviour to realize that it contrasted strangely with his former adoring reverence. Her annoyance increased now; she didn't want his unselfish devotion; but he had no right to take it away from her – she felt she'd been deprived of something that was really her property and gave him an indignant glance.

How dare he inflict his sulks and silence upon her – so childish and stupid? He had no business to be sitting there – he ought to have vanished. If she'd really possessed magic powers, her venomous glance would have disintegrated the handsome young man on the spot. At such close quarters she found his nearness oppressive, he seemed to occupy too much room. Though she didn't know it, his physical presence threatened the derealizing process on which she depended for her peace of mind. He seemed overpowering physically, rather as if some great snow animal had climbed into the car and were sitting beside her, taking up far too much space. But, though over-assertive, his presence was also lifeless, in its sullen, stupid silence, as though some great *stuffed* animal sat in the driver's seat.

She glanced at him again, in amusement this time, her good humour quickly restored. Of course he was lifeless. He had to be, since he wasn't real but a character she had dreamed up, no more important to her than the memory of the pony, Coffee.

Nestling into the comforting warmth and softness of her fur coat, closing her eyes, she settled down to wait for the drive to end, oblivious of Oswald and of her surroundings. She had no further use for the north, its spell had broken, for good and all this time. She simply waited to be somewhere else.

She took no notice of the storm when it broke at last, just as they turned inland, the booming clouds releasing torrents of pale snow or sleet, in which were entangled odd electrical flickerings, which might have been lightning, or the aurora borealis, or Jove's thunderbolts – she didn't care which they were, she was indifferent, and scarcely looked.

*

It wouldn't have interested her to know how persistently the man beside her was being tormented all the time by all sorts of painful emotions, of which she was the centre. His mental state was still far from normal, although to a point he had regained control. The satisfaction of his desire had brought him no peace, his senses were in a ferment, his thoughts churning distractedly in his head.

Of his behaviour at Bannenberg he refused to think. The memory of what he'd done there was insupportable and had left an aftermath of disgust and shame he tried to transfer to

Rejane, blaming her for all he had suffered and was suffering now. The whole time he had loved her it had been torture, and now that his love had turned to hate, the torture was ten times worse. That she should be unapproachable, like a princess, he'd been able to bear as long as she represented his dream and been glorified by its nameless brightness, because, paradoxically, it identified her with him.

Now all this was changed: her perfection had gone, and so had his worship. He still hadn't got over the shock of seeing the undisguised witch-look on her face, showing him that he'd been deluding himself, and that she cared nothing for him, had nothing to do with his dream. Now he saw her without that mysterious brightness, and he couldn't bear what he saw; though, really, when he thought he was seeing her objectively, it was through the dark veil of all his other suppressed grievances. He had thrown himself upon her with such brutal violence because he'd felt wronged in the regiment, because his comrades had turned the cold shoulder upon him, because he'd been persecuted by their wives.

When the storm broke and the road veered away from the dangerous cliffs, he knew, by the pang of disappointment that went through him, that he must really have been hoping for a catastrophe, and that the car would become their coffin. He now really wanted to cut himself altogether from the unjust world and the love by which he had been betrayed. His silence – which had lasted so long that it seemed impossible to break – was a manifestation of this death-wish, which, however, he did not recognize for what it was.

In connection with himself, the whole concept of death seemed unreal; in his healthy extrovert existence, always fully occupied, he'd never thought about it. Even his father's death long ago had made no impression on him. His temperament, background and education prevented him from viewing his own death as an aim he might achieve by his own action. Hence his disappointment because the sea and the storm failed to achieve it for him.

All the same, without knowing what he was doing, he continued to proceed towards his objective by devious methods, indirectly, by concentrating on all that was most painful to him and made his life seem not worth while.

He kept telling himself that, to Rejane, he could have been only a casual pick-up, a convenience, of whom she had made use because nobody else happened to be on hand. Their relationship could have meant no more to her than any trivial holiday episode. But what an atrocious thing it was to play on a man's deepest feelings as she had! First she'd made him ashamed of his restraint; then of his brutal outburst of passion; and finally she'd deprived him of his revenge by throwing herself into his arms – what depravity, to give the situation that fiendish twist! And he, instead of retaliating in the only possible way, by rejecting her utterly, had weakly submitted, allowed her to make use of him to gratify her lust. Could anything be more contemptible than the part he had played?

As wave after wave of humiliation swept over him, he tried to distract himself from his own shame by the violence of his raging against her. What a devil of a woman she was, turning him into something he never had been, a sadistic ravisher, just in order to give herself a perverted thrill! How she must have been laughing at him all the time, pretending she was a sweet young girl, when really she was this . . . corrupt horror . . . this abomination. . . .

Here his normal sense of fairness rebelled, reminding him that he himself was not blameless by any means. At once, as the memory began to force itself on him, his whole being recoiled in horror from what he had done. The memory of that sadistic act, totally opposed to all his deepest beliefs, was unendurable, simply – he slammed the doors of his mind, he couldn't bear to think of it or to know about it.

If only he'd never set eyes on Rejane! Even while he was thinking this, he gave her a furtive glance, and what he saw struck him a fresh blow.

Her whole natural, artless pose, and particularly the way her head, thrown back and resting against the seat, jolted with the jolts of the car, seemed to express youthful pathos and innocence, like a tired child fallen asleep on a journey. All the abuse he'd been piling upon her was now heaped on his own head in self-reproach, as he realized that, whatever happened, some part of him would always see her as the adorable young girl he had loved with so pure and fervent a love.

But this picture was the very opposite of the new one he'd set up in his mind, where the two contradictory images seemed to exist side by side, the gentler more idealized version persisting, no matter how viciously he tried to destroy it. She really might have bewitched him, for nothing could stop the frantic racing of his crazy, discordant thoughts for a single second.

It was the time of the long-drawn-out twilight, not quite dark enough for the headlights, though a slow dissolution was setting in, the familiar everyday world dissolving out of existence. Peering out as he drove, Oswald felt a confused longing for peace – for the quiet gravity and stillness of the hour, so characteristically northern, to extend its influence to his brain. But everything seemed different today, the peaceful charm of the dusk infiltrated by something malevolent, evil. Though objects still retained their usual forms, they gave the impression of being about to change into more sinister shapes, in a world gone grey and uncanny, as if disembodied. Suddenly he had the crazy notion that the malevolence he seemed to feel in the air came from the woman beside him, who seemed to be everywhere, outside as well as within him. The stony road, those trees, that rock, the steering-wheel, his own hands upon it, all were poisoned, permeated by her, because they were perceived by his senses, where she had established herself, to reside for ever.

To his obsessed imagination, it seemed that a part of her had, in some diabolical way, entered into him while she lay in his arms – a sucker, or a tentacle, through which she could always feed, vampire-like, on his living essence. How unspeakable! What a horror!

Appalled, clenching both hands on the wheel, he felt his whole body stiffen with the horror that tightened each nerve. At this moment a tree loomed up ahead, and, instead of following the curve of the road, he drove straight at it, though still without recognizing the suicidal impulse. His unclear thought was that his horror was so great that it must extend to the car, which, in consequence, would insist on leaving the road, crashing into the tree and smashing itself to pieces. At that speed, the violent wrench with which he, at the last moment, kept the car on the road, almost capsized it. After lurching dangerously, it righted itself, shaving narrowly past the three, while the tips of the dangling branches scraped the roof like sharp fingernails.

This peculiar thin, scratching sound seemed to recall Oswald to himself. Even now he didn't see his real object, merely telling himself he must be mad to take such risks for no reason. Slowing down for a moment, he pressed his hand to his head, trying to clear his thoughts, and, while he did so, his unguarded face looked boyish again, lost, bewildered and touching.

Then, resuming his stern military mask, he switched on the headlights and settled down resolutely to finish the drive speedily and safely, keeping his eyes away from Rejane with a deliberate effort, thankful she didn't ask what had happened.

Though the lurch and the queer scraping noise of the twigs had brought her out of her dreams she'd merely blinked sleepily at the light jumping from tree to tree, then closed her eyes again, feeling that, now that darkness had fallen, this endless drive was like an illness she might as well sleep through, since she had to endure it. When next she looked out, the white double drive of The Hope Deferred was opening ahead like welcoming outspread arms, and she exclaimed in delight, 'Why, we're here!' The memory of Oswald's uncivilized conduct was now recalled to her – she'd forgotten all about it, insignificant detail that it was – by the absence of any response.

Actually, at her spontaneous exclamation, the man felt an overwhelming wave of love. The old charm still worked, he could hardly resist, even now. He was worn out, so exhausted in body and mind that he longed only to give way to her, not to struggle any more. What bliss it would be just to put his head in her lap and feel her hand on his hair! With a sensation of being pulled apart, he reminded himself of what she really was, told himself that the spell was an evil one, the naturalness a fake.

'If anyone asks, I shall say you slipped on the rocks and that I fell trying to help you' was all he said, in a voice that sounded to him unnatural, stiff with disuse.

'Say whatever you like,' she replied indifferently, running up the steps without looking round at him.

He knew he ought to drive off at once. Yet somehow he found himself following her into the hall, as if pulled after her against his will. He saw the manager come hurrying forward, glancing with instantly suppressed astonishment at her sea-stained clothes, saying, 'We were getting anxious. . . .' The man's curiosity was odious to him. But she went on her way unperturbed, seeming not to notice, simply waving an airy hand towards him, indicating that he would explain their late arrival.

'And please have them send me up something to eat – I shan't come down again.' She spoke with finality, dismissing them both as of equal status, with a civil, impersonal 'Goodnight', just before she vanished, like an employer bestowing a tip.

As he watched her disappear, for a second the young officer really felt as if he would die unless he ran after her, threw himself at her feet and implored her to spend this last evening with him. The insult of her voice and manner passed over his head, unnoticed.

Then, collecting himself, he approached the manager, spoke a few words of explanation, and, without waiting to see how they were received, marched out to the car again and set off for home. Deadly tiredness had overwhelmed him like the sudden onset of influenza. He hardly knew what he was doing, only conscious within himself of the emptiness, the shame and the disappointment – the detritus of his own utter failure, both as a lover and as a man.

At this hour the road he knew so well was deserted, and he fell, as he drove, into frequent blank spots, like sleeps, when nothing registered with him; emerging from one of these to find himself crossing the humpback bridge and in sight of his destination. Longing for the sanctuary of his own room, the privacy and relief of sleep that would not be disturbed, he drove up the last steep incline to his home.

6

THE family had never owned a car. Since cars came into general use, there had never been enough money to buy one. So there was no proper garage. Oswald used the old coach-house, facing the back door across a wide, cobbled courtyard. He installed the car here, went out and shut the heavy door, meaning to lock up and then go indoors. But, in a trance, almost, of weariness, after turning the big heavy old-fashioned key in the lock, he stood with it in his hand, leaning against the door in the dark.

He was as he remembered being only once or twice before in his life, after some exceptionally exhausting exercise, too tired to move or even to think. His present tiredness had the useful effect of blocking memory as well, so that he need know nothing about what had happened at Bannenberg.

The effort of driving had kept him awake, more or less. But now that he was standing still doing nothing but lean against the door, his eyes started to close. Oblivion seemed to catch hold of him and to draw him out of his body with soft, clinging, irresistible hands. Dreaming already, asleep on his feet, he seemed to see the high, yellow-wheeled dogcart his father had driven, which was one of his earliest memories. 'There'll soon be some skating,' he told himself, trying to think back to his boyhood and to lose himself in his dream.

He was growing colder and colder, but he still didn't move, weariness and discomfort mingling in one vast, all-embracing grievance, heavily tinged with self-pity. Surely he was at least entitled to the privacy of his own room. Longing to shut himself in there and go to sleep, he dimly saw himself as being like some hunted animal, persecuted by men and by its own kind, wanting only to crawl into its lair, unmolested and unobserved.

*

A moment later, the back door opened, releasing a stream of yellow light, not quite bright enough to reach across the courtyard to where he was standing.

'Oswald?'

The young man heard his sister's voice call his name, but, in his abnormal state, saw no necessity to answer – she belonged to the hostile conspiracy against him. In silence he watched her looking round, not seeing him yet, peering from inside the door, evidently reluctant to come out into the cold in her flimsy, short-sleeved dress. It was one she often wore in the evenings, with a full skirt and a flowery pattern of roses. He had seen it dozens of times without taking much notice, and had no idea why it now inspired in him an irrational annoyance. That she changed only at night because the concession to gentility pleased their mother didn't affect his irritation at seeing the big, quiet, serious girl wearing a dress more suited to somebody frivolous and lively.

Why can't she see she's just making herself ridiculous? he thought, as if this was why he didn't attempt to communicate with her. But then a more natural impulse made him step forward, moving his chilled body with difficulty, his legs stiff, his feet clattering on the cobbles like lumps of iron.

'So it's you.' Vera's voice sounded both curious and censorious. 'What are you doing out here? Why don't you come indoors?'

He could tell that, even before she'd really seen him, she knew something was wrong, and he longed to get into the house without having to talk to her. But her tall figure in the absurd, full, flowery dress almost filled the doorway and left him no room to pass. Still locked in a silence too difficult to break, he advanced into the light and, planting himself in front of her, stood there without opening his mouth: while she stared at him in amazement, exclaiming, 'Heavens! What's happened to you? Has there been an accident?'

To Oswald, her gaze seemed to jump out of her eyes – he could feel it running all over him from head to foot, investigating, with eager stealth and speed, every defect in his appearance, noting it in some invisible inventory, from which she would later deduce the whole story of his adventures. Her furtive, avid manner of conducting this swift examination was immediately, immensely repulsive to him. To avoid looking at her, he lowered his own eyes to the cobbles; which at once became identical mounds of sand, strongly lit on one side by theatrical sunset light, in a desert where he was wandering, nameless and lost. Then he was astonished to see, in a trough of darkness between two of the dunes, a tuft of dry, withered grass growing; and at once he was himself again, everything sprang back into its true perspective.

But what on earth had gone wrong with him? Why was he seeing things as they were not? He felt, for a second, really alarmed by his alien thoughts and illusions, which seemed outside his control and liable, at any moment, to escape from his skull (if they hadn't done so already) in the form of actions equally uncontrollable. The shock made him pull himself together. When Vera asked again, 'What't the matter? What's happened to you?' he replied clearly and firmly: 'Nothing. Nothing's happened. Except that I slipped and fell down. . . .'

There was an infinitesimal pause, during which he realized that he couldn't possibly hope to get off so lightly. He would have to say something more, offer an explanation.

'You know what the place is like inside,' he said with difficulty, dangerously skirting the fringe of forgotten events. 'How dark and slippery it is. . . .'

Closer than this he dared not go, already feeling the heave of some intolerable thing, struggling to break through into consciousness. Clenching his fists with the effort of not knowing what it was, he hurried on. 'I don't want Mother to see me like this.' His sensation was of having come to the very edge of a frightful precipice, from which he'd stepped back only just in time. Thinking more of this than the words, he'd already said, 'After all the fuss this morning she's bound to imagine the worst', before the remembered echo of his own brutal voice speaking then silenced him abruptly. It was hopeless to expect Vera's co-operation. She always had been against him, and now he'd given her real cause for resentment.

The last thing he expected was to hear her say kindly, 'You look dead tired. Why not go straight up to your room? I'll keep Mother out of the way and bring you something to eat after she's gone to bed.'

He glanced at her with instinctive distrust but softened at once, seeing on her face a forgotten look of secret complicity, with which as children they used to help one another out of their various scrapes, in league together against adult authority. It brought him a sudden swift warmth, a glimpse of the golden glow of perpetual sunshine lighting that happy childhood world he had shared with her.

'Thanks, V. That's jolly decent of you.' Without knowing it, he fell automatically into the idiom of that innocent, carefree, lost period; immeasureably more lost to him than yesterday – the thought shot, cometlike, through his head, trailing dangers at which he refused to look. He looked at his sister instead, and, noticing the goose-flesh of her bare arms, was momentarily touched.

But childhood's radiance was already fading. And now her hungry, expectant glance extinguished it altogether and alienated him afresh. Though she asked no questions, her curiosity was to be felt, all the more noticeable because it came out of her silence and sympathy. Her eyes kept turning towards him, full of hateful inquisitiveness, and of a mute urgent appeal of some sort, incomprehensible to him – it was no concern of his. All that concerned him was their curiosity, which seemed to delve into him, searching about for his secrets in a way that was dangerous and repulsive, though he was too tired to know just where the danger lay.

Becoming exasperated in his exhaustion, with a sense of giving up the struggle, he thought, I simply can't stand those flowers another second, allowing his irritation to swamp everything. Then he pushed past the offending dress and went into the house, through which he could have found his way blindfold, hurrying up the back stairs in the dark, and along the familiar passages to his room, where he thankfully shut himself in.

The large, cold, bare room, though it had always been his, was oddly impersonal, scrupulously clean and tidy, his few simple possessions grouped neatly and with a sort of unconscious pathos, as if ready for instant departure from a temporary encampment, where he would not stay long enough to justify any attempt at comfort.

It was the sanctuary for which he had longed, and for a moment its severe plainness had a restorative effect. But this soon wore off, and he became aware that something was wrong, making him restless and uneasy. He'd shut out of his mind the obscure threat of Vera's curiosity as he shut the door; but something infinitely more disturbing had entered with him. Though he didn't know what it was, deep within him his unacknowledged shame was making itself felt – suddenly the austerity of the room seemed to reproach him. He felt he defiled it in his filthy clothes. With loathing, he tore them off, bundled them up together.

But then he didn't know what to do with them, he was at a loss. His instinct was to destroy the things; he'd have liked to push them into the kitchen stove. But he was afraid of meeting his mother or sister if he left his room, and that there would be more questions. As he stood there in his pyjamas, holding the bundle, his fair, fine, disordered hair made him look a boy, his face touchingly young, tired and bewildered.

Asleep, almost, on his feet, he was at his wits' end, unable to evolve the simplest plan. Finally, in desperation, he threw the bundle across the room and fell into bed, unconscious even before his head was on the hard pillow.

*

Oswald never stirred when his sister came in a little while with a tray of food. She looked at the handsome, blond young fellow lying there, lost and drowned in sleep, dead to the world, and saw that he was not to be roused. As she was going out again, she noticed the bundle of clothes on the floor; and her face, which had been muted and rather sad, sharpened in that curiosity her brother found so repulsive. She stooped to investigate, pulling the bundle open a little; then, still with the same hungry, inquiring expression, took it away with her, closing the door softly so as not to disturb the sleeper.

It would have taken a far louder noise than that of a door to wake him just then. Sleep was his vital need, and he had to have it. It was his one possibility of escape from an insupportable situation. If only he could go on sleeping until he was back on duty again and his troubles were over, was his last thought, as he had the impression of hurling himself deliberately into the black abyss opening to receive him.

In the morning, instead of coming fully awake as usual, in possession of all his faculties, as at the sound of a ghostly bugle, he woke reluctantly, climbing laboriously and against his will out of the dark gulf where he had lain without moving the whole night long. If only he need not wake but could remain there, ignorant and innocent, as he'd been in his sleep! But it was no use wishing, already he was back again in his life. Before he'd even opened his eyes, he felt the events of yesterday lying in wait for him. He remembered, and pressed his eyelids together to shut out the light, unwilling to face the shame of existing.

However, the intervening hours of sound sleep had fulfilled their function, removing the actuality of Bannenberg a little from him. The guilty horror was slightly less immediate; he could think of it now as he could not have done before.

Yesterday he had refused absolutely to admit that passion had made him act like a wild animal. Now, though it was still torture even to glance at the fact, he saw that, if ever he was to be reconciled to himself, he would have to accept the truth and learn to endure it. He even saw dimly that this might be possible. Eventually. But not yet. The thing was too recent. The memory too agonizing, too raw.

Even the partial recognition, which was all he could so far achieve, had already, during these first waking moments, filled him with such sick self-disgust, such distaste for living, that he didn't know how he was to go on. How could he bear his existence, through all the years stretching ahead? If only he could have stayed asleep! But the black abyss, into which he had plunged last night, now seemed quite out of his reach, not to be attained until it closed over his head for ever. And what a long dreary time of misery he would have to live through first!

As it had to be lived through, because he had to remain alive, he must forget about what he had done. He took this for granted, as if he couldn't possibly be required to face life in full consciousness of his guilt. He couldn't endure it, no man could, it would not be expected of him. So, as a temporary expedient only, he again thrust the memory of Bannenberg out of sight, down into the deepest depths of himself. He did it because he must, if his life must go on.

He looked round the room, instinctively seeking some well-known reassurance that had always been there before, but today, when most needed, was unaccountably not forthcoming. An indefinable air of estrangement about the walls and the familiar objects around him transformed him into a stranger in their midst. He was no longer at home here. Oppressed by his reluctance to start the day, to take up the burden of living again, he was still lying in bed; and this unprecedented sloth made him feel even more of a stranger to himself, and to all around him.

Because he'd just ceased to remember yesterday with any distinctness, at first he didn't think of his clothes. But when he noticed that the bundle had gone, the shock roused him effectively. Jumping out of bed, he looked quickly around, making sure that the things were not anywhere in the room; then, hurriedly, automatically, he started to dress, his mind all the while gripped separate in apprehension. He couldn't ask himself why he was so disturbed by the bundle's disappearance without reviving his guilty shame, of which he was now aware only as the numbed pain of an internal wound, bearable as it was, but liable to become agonizing again at the least touch – at a glance even. It must at all costs be shielded, hidden; his whole being seemed to turn inwards and close round it protectively, to keep it secret. Nobody must know about it, or even guess it was there.

He knew the bundle was somehow connected with this shameful secret wound. Could it lead to its exposure? His obscure dread was that it might in some way betray his secret. What a fool he had been not to lock his door against Vera's detestable curiosity, for of course she must have taken the things. Full of animosity towards her, the moment he was ready he ran downstairs, knowing he'd find her in the kitchen, preparing breakfast, before their mother came down.

*

The first thing he saw there when he opened the door was the missing garments, clean and pressed, hanging neatly over the back of a chair. Unprepared for this, he was taken aback, and stood staring, while Vera explained, without leaving the stove, how she hadn't disturbed him the night before but had brought down his clothes to clean them while their mother was out of the way.

Oswald thanked her uncomfortably, thinking that no one could have been kinder, more helpful. Why wasn't he grateful? Why did he still feel unfriendly? Dimly he perceived that it wasn't only that he distrusted Vera – he didn't want the contact of friendliness with her or with anyone. He who had always been sociable and warm-hearted, was shut off alone, in the dark enclosure of himself. He wondered at it a little without understanding, feeling isolated as he had never been.

All at once, he knew his sister's eyes were upon him and he looked at her. Although she averted them hurriedly, he'd already caught their sidelong, searching glance of sharp, hungry curiosity, which infuriated and frightened him like a glimpse of the devil.

'What are you staring at?' he asked, coldly hostile. A sort of frenzied suspicion surged up in him. She seemed to be trying to uncover his secret wound, round which he clutched himself still more tightly, standing there rigid, tense with exasperation; while she remained silent, her face turned from him, hurt by the way he had spoken.

In reality, she was a pathetic person. She'd seen her fate clearly when her two sisters left home, doomed to stay there as long as her mother lived, and had forced herself to accept the position. But she couldn't force herself not to resent her frustration in life and love, or not to be ashamed of her ignorance, which she felt was degrading. Since she was to be denied the experience of passionate love, someone should at least tell her something about it, to save her from the ignominy of her absolute ignorance. And only Oswald could do so – she couldn't possibly ask her mother. Always brooding, the obsessed girl had come to believe that he knew of the craving, tormenting her all the time, worse than an aching tooth. Surely he couldn't be so heartless as to leave it unsatisfied?

By speaking kindly to her for a moment when he came home last night he had raised her hopes. In the midnight silence, working over his clothes, she'd made an imaginary bargain with him, persuading herself that, in return, he would tell her something of those mysteries she was longing to share. There must be a connection between his love affair and the stains she was patiently sponging away; so here was a ready-made opening, the subject would come up naturally, of itself.

When he merely asked angrily what she was staring at, she felt defrauded. It seemed most unkind, most unfair. Driven by her desperate desire for the information he cruelly seemed to deliberately withholding, she asked him how he'd got into such a mess – anyone would think he'd been in the sea. All her pathetic yearning was in her eyes as she put this leading question, begging him to save her from a lifetime of feeling inferior to other women.

But he thought she was searching for his secret wound with those imploring eyes, which to him were importunate, impudent and intrusive – intolerably spying. His secret was locked inside him, safe as long as it was left alone. But if she kept on peering and prying, something might come to light; which was unthinkable. He shuddered at the possibility of his raw, wincing wound exposed to her indecent inquisitiveness. She ought not to have even suspected its existence. No longer seeing her as his sister, who shared precious memories of the past, he wanted to thrust her away, slash her out of his sight. He had to hold himself in, clenching his fists as he stood, biting his lips, without saying a word.

Each enclosed in a private obsession, the pair confronted one another like figures under glass domes who could never possibly come together. The girl had no way of knowing that the fair, fine-looking, soldierly young man before her was imprisoned in a very dark place where he couldn't even see her. But she at last realized from his attitude that he would never tell her the things she was dying to know. It seemed to her a callous disregard of her urgent need; base ingratitude, after she'd worked half the night on his clothes. She was stung into an attempt at retaliation.

'I suppose you quarrelled with your girl-friend, and that's why you looked so glum last night. Did she push you into the water?' Half frightened by her own audacity, feeling she was going too far, she couldn't quite bring off the sneer.

Her brother still didn't speak, merely giving her a long,

stern, frigid, outraged look, as if to oppose her obscene curiosity with his eyes, until he'd extinguished it.

Unable to meet that cold, blue, insulting stare, she turned back to the stove. But, the next moment, seeing him on his way to the door, she called after him, feeling goaded: 'You're going to her now, aren't you? Crawling back like a smacked pup . . . it's disgusting . . . you might at least wait till after breakfast . . .', her voice expiring in an undignified sob.

But he was no longer aware of her, or of what she was saying. He had moved with instinctive decision, knowing only that he must get away from her and from everything here. This had become his one aim and object, and he kept on, deeply preoccupied with his inner need to avoid all contact, along the flagged passage and into the yard, not giving Vera a thought. While she stood, crushed by the final affront of his going without a word, as though she were beneath his notice, tears overflowing her eyes unheeded, hearing the coach-house door open, the car start up and drive away.

When her mother called to her from another room she didn't answer, but, angrily drying her eyes, thought with indignation, Off he goes, and leaves me to do all his dirty work as usual. Now she would have to cope with the old lady, pacify her, invent some plausible excuse for Oswald's behaviour.

Yet she didn't really resent it particularly, for in this he was only exercising his masculine privilege, as was to be expected.

7

NO more conscious of where he was going than of the distress he had caused his sister, Oswald drove for a time in a curious, neutral, blank state. When he suddenly noticed the moor, all very bare and grey, stripped to the bone for winter, under the leaden and lowering sky, it was with a shock like surprise. Why was he on this road – the road to The Hope Deferred?

While he slept, that part of him which was concerned with his adjustment to life had decided he must not see Rejane again; and, consciously, he'd made up his mind to telephone an excuse for not coming to say goodbye in person. Now, at first, he thought merely that he'd had to escape from his home, where there was no peace, no security for him. Yet, even as he felt the appropriate bitterness, he knew that his was not the real explanation – his thoughts seemed not to be what he was really thinking.

Having perceived this, he went on to perceive that the same principle applied to everything, outside as well as within him. Even the moor he'd known and loved all his life appeared changed and unreal. Even his army career, which had been more important than anything to him, had become an illusion; and what was left of his world he couldn't imagine. His vague impression was that it had collapsed, and that he was lost in the debris, the general débâcle.

When he saw the familiar double drive and the hotel ahead, he realized all at once that he'd been drawn here helplessly, with no say in the matter. He had, simply, to see Rejane. Nobody, nothing else really existed; it was her absence that made his world seem unreal, for she was his only reality.

Pulling up sharply a little way from the entrance, he sat for a moment, motionless, while this sank in. In all the world, she alone was real and had definition. Everything else was illusion. And she was about to leave him. He sat as if stunned. Then, collecting himself quickly, glancing about to see if he'd been observed, he hurriedly left the car and went into the building.

His thoughts and emotions were all in chaos. He couldn't tell whether love or hate was making his hand shake so that he could hardly open the door of her room, though his training in discipline kept him very correct and calm outwardly, his magnificent soldier's figure almost at attention, as he stood before her.

After his conduct, and the general nightmare of yesterday, she had neither wished nor expected to see him again. But now she was in such high spirits because she was going back to her own world that nothing mattered; nothing could affect her happiness. She gave him a radiant smile of pure joy because she was leaving him and all this gloomy northern interlude for ever. She even said, 'I'm glad you came over to say goodbye.'

She seemed even more beautiful than he'd remembered. In spite of his disillusionment and the efforts he'd made to destroy his love, her beauty still held him enthralled. The sound of the word goodbye caused him an anguish so acute that it wrung from him the exclamation, 'How could I possibly *not* have come?' His eyes burned fever bright, and, as he spoke, he extended his arms curiously in a tortured movement, as if he were on the rack, of which he knew nothing, only amazed by the note of open avowal he heard in his own voice – so it was love, not hate, in the end.

He watched her, bemused; he was as though mesmerized by her loveliness, which her happy excitement increased by the faintest flush, so that she had the perfection of a pale rose. The very air about her seemed scented and full of light. He took deep breaths of the perfume he loved; and, as though it were intoxicating, or possessed magic powers, a remarkable change came over him. His splendid body seemed to come more alive, the expression more animated on his handsome young face. All of a sudden, he really had that officer-in-a-crack-regiment's air of light-hearted assurance and of carrying all before him, which had always belonged to his aura but previously been in abeyance. Suddenly smiling and debonair, he proposed to drive her to catch the boat-train, sweeping aside arrangements already made with such smiling confidence that she looked at him in surprise.

Emerging briefly from her dream of departure, she coolly and shrewdly surveyed the young man who was directing the hotel staff with this new sort of aplomb, as if he expected to be obeyed by everyone to the end of time. This was as he should always have been. Yet to her at least there was something faintly unnatural about the performance; it was not quite convincing. He was giving orders about her things, smiling and irresistible, as if to the manner born. But his brilliant blue eyes had a crazy sparkle, and, with the lock of whitish hair falling between them, in spite of all his correctness, he looked strange – wild and reckless, feverish; almost a bit demented. She could see through this reckless wildness to the helpless despair beneath. At the back of his crazily glittering eyes was the pathos of a blank lost look, which told her she had nothing to fear from him. As far as she was concerned he was finished – his day was done. He was only a sort of phantom to her from the past; no need to believe he was real for an instant. Back she slipped into her happy dreaming again, already far distant from him, as, with queer, smiling, unnatural ease he escorted her from The Hope Deferred for the very last time.

Oswald himself was rather puzzled by this access of unexpected assurance. Where could it have come from? But he was glad to accept it and to let it sweep him along. As long as it lasted, he felt bound to get his own way, as if he had made a pact with the devil; or as if the black threat of loss hanging over him brought this strange compensation of confidence which was almost a touch of madness.

In the car he continued to be animated, refusing to think of either the past or the future, cutting off his perceptions deliberately, trying to limit them to each moment as it came, and to the small, familiar, moving enclosure where he was alone with the woman he loved. The attempt was only partly successful: though he wouldn't admit it, some part of him never ceased being aware of what each passing moment was bringing nearer. Darkness and loss were advancing, implacable as the night.

At the station he would not see beyond Rejane's beauty, which, like a lighted lamp, illuminated the grey, bitter day and the drab platform. Nevertheless at the back of his mind he was aware that the darkness was closing in. The train was due to leave immediately, and, having installed her in it, he got out and stood stiffly, as if on guard, gazing up at her window.

She was wearing her fur coat, and, though he hadn't noticed it specially so far, he now saw how the dusky, soft, luxurious coat, made of the skins of many little dead animals, accentuated her living beauty. Its bulk made her seem smaller and frailer, almost like a fragile little girl. A pang went through him, unendurable – how could he be parted from her and live? Again he unconsciously stretched his arms in that peculiar tortured gesture. While the train suddenly shuddered along all its length, all the hairs of the small dead animals trembled, as if with returning life; and the man also trembled, and his life seemed to pause. Darkness was upon him.

With that night descending, he heard his voice speak again, but most strangely, out of the dark, stricken depths: 'I can't bear to see you go.' It was against all his inherited instincts as well as his disciplined training to say such a thing; but nothing mattered now in the darkness where his life hung in suspense.

She called, 'Then come with me – come and see me on to the boat', smiling, not making the suggestion quite seriously, but with a sort of gay challenge, as if saying, 'I dare you to come.'

He had no time to answer before, with a strong heave, the train pulled her away, starting to slide past him, curving and gliding out of the station. Already the engine was out of sight, the bare rails, nakedly gleaming, stretching out longer and longer, while people waved or turned already towards the exits.

Without a thought in his head, the young man watched the last compartment glide past, then, at the very end of the train came the luggage-van, its big sliding doors still open wide as if to welcome him in; as all his splendid muscles effortlessly combined, with perfect co-ordination and timing, to swing him on board.

Two men in uniform, stacking trunks at the back of the van, stared, astounded, as at an angel fallen from heaven, before they began to protest and approach him. As if they were paper men, Oswald pushed them aside, with a strange inhuman assurance, pressing money into their hands, a fixed uncanny grin on his face. Not knowing what to make of it, they stood speechlessly staring, while he crossed the iron connecting-plates, clashing and jerking under his feet, and came to the corridor of the train beyond.

He was still possessed of that unnatural confidence, against which no obstruction could stand. The meaningless shapes and noises fell back and were instantly lost, swallowed up by the roar and rush of the train. Everything clattering and rocking round him, with mad immutable calm he walked down the swaying corridor until he found Rejane's compartment and entered. Light came back to him then, and to the world, his life went on again. At the last moment, he had been reprieved.

The reprieve was only temporary, a poor depreciating investment to set against the bankruptcy of total loss he would still soon have to face. But for the moment he was beyond fate's reach, safe in his charmed assurance, laughing and talking with an animation that was not his own, his eyes brilliant and distracted, feeling unlike himself, rather as though he were slightly drunk.

Rejane glanced at him dubiously now and then, not at all

sure that she wanted him with her. She hadn't expected him to come, really. But his spectacular leap on to the moving train had pleased her vanity; and a handsome man was always a desirable appendage, an accessory to her elegance, and an insurance against any momentary lack of self-confidence. So she accepted him, with certain provisos, for the time being.

*

The short journey was soon over. Masts appeared, like a forest of bare saplings, clustered against the sullen gleam of grey water. Then they were at the station, which was part of the docks, and in the harbour itself.

As Oswald heard the harsh cries of gulls, his assurance abruptly vanished, leaving him unprotected. By the sudden chill that gripped him, he knew he should never have come. Yet he must go through with it now; he was committed.

With automatic efficiency he dealt with porters and luggage. Then, emerging beside Rejane from the echoing station, he was startled by the portentous sight of the liner's great hull just in front of them, looming like the ominous, enormous symbol of inexorable fate, high over their heads.

He felt a sudden hatred for the ship; which increased as he followed Rejane through its warm, lighted interior, hating the comfort which placed it so unmistakably in her world of wealth, where he didn't belong.

The luxury of her stateroom made it seem quite unreal, like a film star's bedroom, softly yet brightly lit. It felt like a hothouse to him, coming straight from the frigid greyness outside, and it was filled like a hothouse with flowers and with their scent – roses, violets, carnations, lilies, camellias, tuberoses, incredibly exotic in the grim north – sent by the lover to welcome her home.

Without knowing where they had come from, Oswald felt an instinctive antipathy to the massed flowers crowding everywhere. There were too many of them, and their scent was too strong, an overpowering sweetness in the warm air.

Noticing how Rejane immediately seemed at home in this atmosphere, which he found merely oppressive, blooming into a new elegance and sophistication, he belatedly began to realize how far her world was removed from his own. For the first time, the power of her money began to dawn on him, as he watched her the centre of a coming and going of immaculate uniforms, a person of importance, while he stood in the background, unnoticed. He'd never really considered the matter till now, when he felt her money pushing him further and further away from her. Suddenly it had come to divide them, like one of the bottomless fiords, with no way of getting across.

She seemed to have forgotten about him already. Unnoticed he stood there, his heart heavy and cold like a stone in his breast, an unwanted onlooker, knowing he ought to leave but unable to drag himself away. His life depended on seeing her, so how could he go?

If only she would ask him to come with her on the boat, as he had on the train! With just the money he happened to have in his pocket, without even a toothbrush, he would follow her gladly to the ends of the earth; and to hell with his family and with the regiment.

When, presently, she merely asked him to come to one of the bars for a parting drink, everything seemed to go dark in a fearful premonition of loneliness, for without her only darkness was left in the world. She walked ahead of him along a softly carpeted corridor, and he had the cruel illusion that she was diminishing in the distance while he was left far behind.

He felt quite alone in the crowded bar, where there were too many smiling faces, as there had been too many flowers. He was so close to her that his hand touched her dress. But the Rejane he knew and loved had already left him. A stranger seemed to inhabit her flawless beauty.

He willed her desperately to come back, staring fixedly at her with spellbound eyes. But she kept her head turned away, talking to the steward behind the bar, and refused to look at him. It was her voice he heard. But she was not speaking. She had left him and gone away.

Yet those were her hands; the hands that had lately picked berries and mushrooms with him, held the reins, patted the pony's neck, fed it with lumps of sugar. It seemed incredible now that they should have done these things. With a certain horror he watched them, flashing with many rings, darting in alien, airy gestures. They were hers – and they were not hers. He had a sensation of nightmare.

She was not coming back to him. Now he had to know it. She had gone too far away. He had lost her – this was the end. Out of the darkness rushing in on all sides, struggling to hold it off, despairingly, he spoke her name, 'Rejane', pleading with her for his life.

She glanced at him then with faint artificial surprise, as if she hadn't expected him still to be there. For the last few minutes she had, in fact, been waiting more and more impatiently for him to go. Why couldn't he see that he wasn't wanted and take himself off?

She looked again, and with indignation, at the fine, soldierly man whose glittering eyes were all the time fixed on her in an Ancient Mariner stare. He was a weight upon her. She longed to be relieved of the burden of his presence, which, though she didn't know it, represented the cruel and frightening north, of which she'd so nearly become the victim. She had thrust the terrifying experience out of her thoughts. But she couldn't relax fully, she couldn't be reabsorbed into her own world, while he was there, as its symbol. She wouldn't feel really safe from the power of the north until she'd got rid of him.

She told herself she could stand no more of his silent gloom. Yesterday, circumstances had forced her to endure it – how dare he try to inflict it on her today as well! She wasn't going to put up with it any longer. He had absolutely no right to be here in her world. He was only a ghost, a shadow, a relic of her finished interlude. Let him go back to the north, where he belonged.

'Don't wait,' she told him brightly, with her malevolent little smile. 'I like my goodbyes short and sweet.' Relieved because she'd dismissed him at last, to make sure there was no misunderstanding, she held out her hand.

*

The man's heart beat once in a heavy down-stroke, then seemed to stop beating. Everything seemed to stop. It grew dark, as if the lights had gone out.

Then, with an emerald flash, as from an evil green eye, her hand, sparkling with rings, came towards him. And, to his surprise, he saw his surroundings unchanged, the lights still shining brightly, the people laughing and talking. Only he was cut off from them now as by the glass wall of an aquarium. They had the remoteness and the slight distortion of things seen through thick glass.

They didn't concern him. But, with a distant anxiety, he watched the hand coming towards him, knowing he wouldn't be able to take it, but not knowing what to do. All contact was ended for him, he could not now bear to touch anyone. He had left all that. He felt a slight horror of the approaching hand: it was coming too close – no one must touch him now.

Suddenly, at the last moment, as if obeying an order only he could hear, he lifted his own hand sharply in a formal salute, bringing his heels together, the other hand stiff at his side; directly afterwards swinging round to make his way out of the room, oblivious of the curious faces that turned to watch him.

People stared, following him with their eyes, but he didn't notice. He had no more to do with them. He had left their bright world, which claimed reality through the illusion of daylight. His love, too, had been an illusion, and he left it behind him with all the rest. All he wanted now was to be quiet.

The lights were too bright here, there were too many people, and they made too much noise. He had to be alone somewhere, undisturbed.

8

TAKING no notice of anyone, Oswald left the ship, leaving his life behind there, as he might have left a dropped glove, and, knowing nothing about it, returned to the station and got into the waiting train. Alone like a dreamer, neither feeling nor thinking anything, he sat in the cold, empty carriage, staring straight in front of him. When bells rang presently and there was the low, lugubrious hoot of a siren, these noises meant nothing to him, had no associations.

Then people began to trickle, to pour into the station, talking cheerfully, walking briskly in the cold air, entering and filling the train. The sight of them roused him a little, making him aware again of being cut off and alone, separated from everyone else. All these others were in the big bright unreal place he'd left. He could not possibly communicate with them, or have anything to do with them.

Nevertheless he wished they would go away. Their presence caused him a distant uneasiness. He didn't look at them, but, with a faint shadowing of anxiety, simply sat waiting till they should have gone. And, though the train was full, nobody came to sit near him.

People looked into his compartment and then hurried on, frightened off by some emanation of loneliness enclosing him like a capsule – the loneliness of one who has gone beyond time and reality – which made them nervous, without knowing why, so that they kept away.

The train started. Sitting quite still and passive, unthinking, Oswald let it carry him back to the small town where he had left the car, got out here, and went into the streets.

It was lunch-time, there were few people about. Those he saw were like dream people, utterly disconnected from him. Yet it was he who felt shadowy beside them – they were solid with life. He vaguely wondered if they could see him, feeling he passed like a shadow, outside their world, and alone. Where was he? What had happened to him? He'd never been like this before. But he was getting used to it and didn't mind. He thought no more about his feelings, or about anything. His consciousness seemed to have left him and gone on somewhere else.

His body, however, continued in its old way, from force of habit. Coming to a restaurant that was almost empty, it went in, ordered and ate a meal, drank some whisky, his real self remaining the whole time aloof. Such things as eating and drinking no longer concerned him, unconcerned as he was with life. But his healthy young body acted out of its own impulse, and, in the same mechanical fashion, began to drive home.

He was like a zombie, a body only, moving about the world, its inner essence already gone. The small part of his brain that still functioned normally was occupied with driving the car. He knew nothing about it when, at a certain crossroads, he swung the wheel right over and drove in a different direction, away from the place where he lived.

*

Now he was on a narrow, neglected by-road, unmarked except on large-scale ordinance maps, and used only by a few adventurous campers and rock climbers, even in summer. Here he passed neither traffic nor houses, driving through country always wilder and more desolate, more given over to water; until he reached a region where the land was reduced to a handful of skeleton fingers pointing between the lochs, treeless, without vegetation of any sort, bare bones of rock reaching out into the blackish water.

On one of these narrow spines running out into the ultimate

desolation of sea and rock, he drove for some time, with a certain fixity of the unconscious will, as to an appointment he had to keep at a given hour, glancing occasionally at his watch, although he'd ceased to register time long ago.

As the short afternoon faded into dusk, one by one the other ridges of land faded out of sight, until he seemed to drive between worlds in a sort of nowhere, no sky, no earth to be seen, only brute crags suddenly looming, and the endless, unstable heave and gleam of the complaining water. The narrow spit of rock was in places little wider than the track, and, though it now and then threw up weird black pinnacles and escarpments, the deep water always pressed close on both sides, as if lying in wait.

With the gathering twilight, snow, which had been in the air all day, started to fall in a sprinkling of frozen grains, like salt out of a shaker. The driver turned a switch so that the windscreen was cleared, but otherwise took no notice – sunshine, wind, rain and snow were alike illusion to him where he was, cut off from himself and from the living world.

Yet, at a point indistinguishable from the rest of this grim solitude, he stopped the car with certainty and precision, though still absent, blank, and sat motionless, letting the windscreen-wipers go on clearing the glass after he'd switched off the engine. He had evidently almost reached the end of the land and the open sea, for, as the engine noise died, the thump of waves rose from the foot of the precipitous drop on the other side of the road. His forgotten sense of responsibility had made him pull up under a mass of rock, which partially shielded the car from the driving snow, already collecting in small drifts and pockets among the boulders.

Nowhere on the way had there been any sign of life, no animal, no sea-bird, even. In this loneliness that was frightening, unutterable, he sat as if waiting for someone, with the outward aspect of having come to an assignation, but blank inwardly, no thought taking shape in his mind.

The sea was turning a more solid black with the approach

of night, only the spray of the breaking waves showing pale through the other whiteness falling out of the sky, which evaporated as it touched them. A strong, erratic wind intermittently sent the snow fuming upwards like smoke, or whirling in crazy spirals along the track. And, with this uncanny luminousness in the air smoking and swirling, the freezing desolate place, seemingly in the void, black fangs of rock jutting sheer out of groaning water, might have represented a northern hell; with the man as one of the damned, on whom everlasting night was descending.

His eyes, always turned to the sea, were still the eyes of a zombie more than a human being. But then there was a change in the static figure. The abnormal blank look left the face, which recovered, in consequence, some of its lost humanity. The eyes focused again.

Not knowing what had alerted him, or what he expected to see, the watcher stared out into the snowy dusk. He had a curious sense of something happening, or about to happen out there which concerned himself; and this, after his prolonged state of absence, seemed strange and almost alarming. He didn't want to return, even in such a limited way, to his conscious self. It was painful, he tried to hold back. But, at the same time, he was aware that an obscure conflict had developed in him where nothing had been, as though he were under an obligation to become conscious.

All at once, leaning forward, he peered more intently through the thin, slanting curtain of snow: in the distance, beyond it, a mirage was forming. In the waste of black waters, mysterious glimmers, like marsh-lights, traced a pattern he half recognized. This was why he had come here – the cluster of small bright stars was what he'd driven so far to see. Startlingly positive and precise, the knowledge burst like a shout in his interior vacuum, which all this time had contained no definite thought.

The sparkling, mysterious, distant stars almost seemed familiar; he almost knew what they were. But not quite. They belonged to his life in the world, to which he no longer had access. He had left it, and now he could not, he didn't even want to go back – it would be too painful. Out of the locked box of his memory nothing came forth.

The twinkling stars were so far away – what could they have to do with him? Yet he felt there was some connection. . . . Slowly, reluctantly, as if compelled, he got out of the car and went to stand at the extreme edge of the precipice, trying to see them more clearly, searching confusedly for something lost, which he must make conscious.

He was so handsome, so young. His magnificent healthy body had hardly been used; it moved with its own spontaneous ease and vigorous youth. But something was missing from the man as a whole which cancelled the fine physique, so that, in spite of his splendid athletic body, he seemed not quite real, not quite there; his expression peculiarly at a loss, a bit deadened, dazed like that of a prisoner in a foreign country, locked in dumb helplessness. Oblivious of the icy wind stinging his skin and tearing at his blond hair, he stood there, imprisoned in his confusion and inner conflict, groping unwillingly after what was lost.

Suddenly he knew he was going to remember. His life seemed to be all around him in the swirling snow. In a moment he would see the stars as they really were, recognize their pattern. No, no – he *could* not! An agony of resistance sprang up in him instantly. The pain of recognition could not be borne. He could not go back to all that. There had been life and love and failure and disappointment; but it was all gone from him now. He was already outside the world – let it remain shut away!

Making no further attempt to recognize or remember, he let his consciousness lapse. As if to abet him, dusk was now deepening into night, blotting out everything. The car, which had been his last link with reality, had already been swallowed up with the rocks beyond. The thud of the unseen waves, rising more ominously in the darkness, was loud in his ears, though it didn't reach his attention, fixed on another sound from far away out there across the water – a sort of mournful low bellowing, a leviathan lamentation.

What could it be? Why should it make him tremble? Though he couldn't prevent these questions from forming, he refused to attend to them, or to associate them with himself. Staring into the falling snow, not in search of the answer to any question, all he saw was the snow-grains ceaselessly swooping at him out of the empty black and, in the distance, the sparkling design of stars.

After all, they were bringing back something from his life in the world . . . a dim recollection of street-lights . . . leading his eyes to where a door seemed to be opening on all his life might have been of nobility and fulfilment. All the love and happiness and success he had never known in his life seemed to shine there, for a moment, against the dark, in the magic light of the resplendent stars.

But then the starry pattern immediately started to change, the stars were changing. Mysteriously dimmed and diminished, they were moving away from him now, with ever-increasing speed, towards the fiord's mouth and the open sea. Already reduced to bright pinpoints, almost out of his sight, they were only a faint, far gleam in the furthest distance. A few more seconds and they would have vanished. He would be alone in the dark.

Profound desolation descended on him as he watched the receding stars. He felt desolate and forlorn, like a child shut out of a bright room, left out of everything. And he longed, with a sudden nostalgic yearning, to be included in life again – in the human family circle. He couldn't bear this exclusion, being shut out in the lonely dark.

But nor could he bear to go back to his life in the world. No, that was not the way. He had come too far already, and could now only go on, further still, away from all he had been.

He would follow the stars before they vanished completely.

The sudden impulse struck with a force that carried him with it . . . onwards . . . forwards . . . away from all the old ache and isolation of consciousness. Parting the snow with his hands like a diver, he pushed the white curtain aside.

And the wave of his destiny, swelling towards a climax, swept him on its forward rush to the climax of breaking; all the elements of his being caught up by the irresistible surge, racing towards dissolution. As he'd plunged into the abyss of sleep, he now abandoned himself to this torrential flood, boundless, impersonal, indistinguishable from the military power to which he was dedicated; hurtling on, in obedience to fate's higher command, further and further from everything, into the unknown.

There follow pages from an original draft
of Anna Kavan's typescript
reproduced in facsimile.

The tall, fine-looking, blond young man who'd just joined the regiment was singularly innocent for his age and era. It wasnt long before somebody in the mess christened him The Parson, and the name stuck, being appropriate; even the men under him used it behind his back. Good tempered and a natural athlete, his popularity was automatic, though his companions teased him a good deal about his chivalrous romantic attitude towards women, and the fact that he prefered not to drink, only doing so to be like them. He took it all in good part, with a wide winning smile that came easily to his otherwise somewhat austere countenance. Only a very few, and those the unpleasantly conceited and supercilious, looked down on him slightly because he came from the far north, and his small remote country was in many ways backward, cut off from the mainstream of continental ideas.

It was traditional there that the eldest son followed in his father's footsteps; which in Oswald's case meant joining this famous regiment, where every young officer had to have some private means. He was one of a family left in poor circumstances by the early death of its head. But, the divine right of the eldest son being traditional too, the rest of them had scraped and stinted themselves to increase his share of the meagre patrimony to the point of providing him with the essential small private income. Ever since he could remember, his mother had slaved and saved for this purpose, skimping the education of her younger sons; the daughters it had not been thought neccessary to educate, beyond the rudiments she herself could teach them. All of which was accepted as perfectly natural by all of them, Oswald included; However, he never forgot his indebtedness, determined to do them credit. And he seemed destined to succeed in his military career, highly thought of by his superiors for his devotion to duty, and his dedicated attitude to the regiment, that belonged to a past generation of soldiers, and was now rare indeed.

There really was something faintly priestlike about him, in spite of his smiling good-fellowship, coming out in his absolute trustworthiness, his conscientiousness and integrity. He wasnt at all dull or priggish, and yet he was distinguished by a curious little air of seriousness that was distinctive and rather engaging, and made him stand out from the rest. The women, particularly, were charmed by it, and made a dead set at him from the first.

The regiment was stationed abroad, and the army wives, living the spoiled, segregated existence of women in tropical lands, had nothing to occupy them but affairs with their husbands' friends, who were delighted to oblige. Only Oswald had no time for them; loayalty would have kept him away from them in any case, but he wasnt attracted. He always treated them all with respectful politeness, remaining firmly aloof; which, contrarily, seemed to excite them, bringing them round him like a swarm of bees.

It became clear to everyone that they were determined to get him. His comrades, amused and half envious, started to bet on his downfall, teasing him more than ever. By now, feeling he was being made ridiculous, he was seriously annoyed by the pestering females who wouldnt leave him alone. They wouldnt be satisfied until he'd surrendered to one of them, <u>which</u> one they no longer cared. The pursuit had started frivolously, as a relief from boredom, but now the chase was in deadly earnest, feminine honor being at stake.

Nothing could have been more repugnant to him than this persecution, and into the bargain he felt a fool. Above all things he loathed the weekly dances all junior officers had to attend, when he felt against his fit muscular body, their soft semi-nakedness, that always seemed to burn, in the tropical heat, with a lustful excitement, repulsive to him beyond words. The abandoned creatures really disgusted him now, But his behaviour was as correct as usual, He danced with each woman in turn, contriving to convey by his attitude, his abysmal lack of interest in any of them, as if he could hardly tell one from another. He developed a knack that was really insulting of holding his partner well away from him like some impersonal piece of equipment he had to drag round the room. As a method of getting his own back it was not unsuccessful. But he had to pay for it in the end.

The men who'd taken the whole thing as a joke, presently ceased to see anything funny in it. The husbands especially